Into the
Faerie Lands

J. R. Bennett

Into The Faerie Lands

Copyright © 2021 by J.R. Bennett

All rights reserved. No part of this publication may be reproduced, distributed, or transmitted in any form or by any means, including photocopying, recording, or other electronic or mechanical methods, without the prior written permission of the author, except in the case of brief quotations embodied in critical reviews and certain other non-commercial uses permitted by copyright law.

Tellwell Talent
www.tellwell.ca

ISBN
978-1-77370-663-4 (Hardcover)
978-1-77370-662-7 (Paperback)
978-1-77370-664-1 (eBook)

Into the
Faerie Lands

To Ms. LaPorte

A former school librarian who put up with my silly ramblings about this faerie land during recess at Hillcrest Public School and whose encouragement allowed for this book to exist.

Chapter I
His Return

~*~

He was dead, that is all everyone knew.

Some people say he died in his sleep, but a twenty-something-year-old dying in their sleep? That's extremely uncommon.

Another theory is that he was murdered, but this idea was dismissed long ago, as he had no enemies. Further evidence to this appeared at his funeral, where reports say the guestbook was full to the brim with signatures.

The truth is that he became horrendously ill and then went missing. One day, as the nurse came to check on his vitals, Edward Worley vanished from his hospital room at St. Christopher's Hospital in Brimley, Ontario, and was never seen again. Search parties were arranged, and nothing was found. Whatever the theory—still alive or dead, and if dead whether it was murder or natural causes—only one fact was certain: Edward (or "Ed") was gone, and that was that.

It was one year after Ed's "death" when a few of his close friends started to receive strange letters.

I am sorry to say that the dates of these events are—and will always remain—unknown to me, however, I can tell you who received these letters. The first person's name was Zacchaeus Dartmouth or, as he preferred, Zach.

Zach was a lanky fellow with straw hair who had been friends with Ed for years. Their relationship was infamous for their verbally-violent arguments over who was mentally superior. Ed once called Zach an "incandescent light bulb," while Zach used even less-friendlier words. However hard they fought, though, they remained friends, and that was how they liked it.

"We good?" Zach once asked of Ed at the end of an exhilarating and long argument.

"We're good." was Ed's blunt reply. "Up yours, but yes, we're good."

It was a cold and dim night when the first letter arrived. Cold drops of rain fell as Zach found the letter in a bundle of bills, and flyers full of pretty people offering a dose of escapism. The envelope was tinted yellow and stamped with a blotch of blue wax with the scent spilled tea on it. The letter ran:

Dear Zach,

I am writing to tell you everything is all right. Don't for a minute worry about me, I'm quite well off. In better health than ever. How is everyone?

Don't tell a soul of this letter, I'll be dealing with it myself.

Warm Regards and other fancy words,

Edward

Zach read these words with a feeling of melancholy. *It can't be him*, Zach thought, *Ed's gone. It must be some sick joke.* He then crumpled the letter into a tight ball and threw it in the recycling and went back to whatever it was he was doing before.

Unnoticed by Zach, a small figure was peering through his living room window. It was around nine inches high, with a head as big and round like a tennis ball. On its face was a pair of big eyes, a little nose and wide mouth that ordinarily would be seen grinning in a mischievous way. It didn't look mischievous this time, however, but rather concerned. It turned around and jumped off the window ledge and puttered to its master waiting in the far distance.

The second letter was delivered to a man named Travis. He and Ed had known each other for years and were practically inseparable in their younger days. Travis was short and was always dying his hair different colours, favouring red highlights against his long black hair at the time of the story. He was born on the reserve in Rama, but spent much of his childhood in Brimley where he and Ed developed their friendship. Unlike Zach, Travis was known for getting Ed into trouble. The two often explored and wandered the world about them, finding themselves, on more than one occasion, being brought home in the back of a police car for trespassing, or for being in the wrong place at the wrong time. So much so, that Travis' parents moved back to the reserve, hoping that exposure to his indigenous heritage would straighten him out.

The note sent to Travis was found in the cushions of his couch. He believed the letter to be true and he even tried to write back. A response came from between the cushions that read:

> *Thank you kindly for writing. The person you have tried to reach is no longer using this post box. Apologies for any inconvenience.*
>
> *– The Imperial Postal Service of the Deltic Empire*

Now, the third letter was given to a girl named Alice. She was a bit older than Ed and only hung around him for a little while. The relationship was platonic at best as Ed was never interested in being with someone. "If I started dating," he would insist, "I wouldn't have any money for books." He and Alice had been close, however, and she was devastated when she heard about Ed's disappearance. This note was found in the mailbox and was nearly taken by a sparrow. It ran:

Dear Alice,

I wish to send you warm wishes but warm wishes are of little necessity at this moment. I have a small request for you. Enclosed along with this letter is a list of persons I would like you to invite to a small party. Some of these names will be familiar to you. Some...not so much. Please make sure that nobody but these people are around.

Best wishes,
Ed

Alice followed the letter's instruction as if it was a final request, but it was met with difficulties. Firstly, due to budget constraints, Alice was forced to host the party at her apartment in Toronto. Secondly, hardly anyone appeared; of all the names on the list, only Zach and Travis showed up for the party. Despite it being a small affair, the group all made the most of it. It had been a long time since any of them had seen each other. Zach had moved to Peterborough and was working on his undergraduate, Travis was working at a shipping plant in Halifax, and Alice was finishing her degree at York and preparing for an internship at an advertising agency. Now there they all were: three friends meeting for the first time in what seemed like forever, with little to say except: "I'm trying to make a start in life."

Alice's room in the house she was renting it from was a modest affair. It was once the living room before being converted some years ago and was of a decent size. A bed huddled in one corner while the other half of the room was neatly made up like a living room under the large front window. One luxury that Alice relished above all was the working fireplace that served as the divide between the *living room* and *bedroom*. "I know a guy from work," she'd say proudly. "He has a property just outside of the city, so I get bushels of wood for cheap."

"Cords," Zach said matter-of-factly.

"What?" Alice inquired, rather confused.

"Wood comes in *cords* not *bushels*," Zach went on hotly as if the term bushel was some sort of transgression against his wellbeing. "You can have a bundle of twigs called a *faggot*, but wood is always in cords."

Alice rolled her eyes and tried to carry the conversation in another direction.

While everyone sat about, chatting and listing to whatever music was playing on the radio, there came a knock at the door. Alice went out to the front door of the house to answer. Upon opening the door, she saw, standing in the cold rain, a young man wearing a trench coat, a long colourful scarf and a wide-brimmed hat with a red velvet carpetbag clutched in one of his hands. She recognized the figure instantly, and out of compulsion kicked him in the shin.

"Ow!" the stranger snapped. "That wasn't very nice."

Alice then hugged the man tightly.

"I can't breathe," hissed the man.

"I don't care," Alice replied, "you're supposed to be dead, Ed."

"Yeah." Ed said, a little more somberly. "I...I can explain. But first, did you follow the letter?"

"Yes."

"Are all the people there?"

"Sort of."

"Pardon?"

"Only Zach and Travis came."

"Bugger all," Ed said, voice heavy with disappointment.

"At least someone showed up." Alice replied, encouragingly.

"Good point." Ed replied, a little more joyfully. "Now, can I come in?"

"No, you can sit out here and catch pneumonia."

"Oh, you're too kind," said Ed sarcastically, and combined a glare with a grin.

Ed was let in. Everyone was surprised when they saw that their old friend was back. Alice had seemed to move from shock to confusion in the time between letting Ed into the apartment. Travis was very much confused; while he wasn't expecting the arrival of his late friend, Travis was more concerned with how Ed pulled it off than his friend's actual resurrection. Zach was cross, as if seeing Ed returning kindled a wave of anger.

"I thought you were dead!" Travis cried.

"You bastard!" Zach snapped. "Wha' the hell do you think you're doin' pretending to be dead like that?"

"I have a lot to explain," answered Ed.

"I'd love to hear it." Zach fired back. "You…you…you lyin' prick!"

Ed pretended to ignore Zach's outburst. "So, to begin," Ed said, after a long sigh, "I would have to go back to a few years ago. I started visiting a fictitious world."

"You were probably dreaming," Zach muttered, but made sure he was heard.

"I wasn't," defended Ed, giving a blunt glare before continuing. "Anyways, I began to settle a home for myself. I became associated with a group known as the *Order of the Four Keepers*. They have helped me begin a life of my own in their world."

"It's a bit of a stretch to believe that," said Zach.

"Well, plug your ears and start hummin'," Ed fired back, "'cause there's more. When I got sick, I found it harder and harder to visit my…we'll call it my *secret garden*. When I was brought to the garden once more, it was to be my last journey from this world. Once I reached there, I had no more strength to go back, so…I stayed. I didn't mean to deceive everyone, but when I was told there was no way I was going to recover, it seemed like the only way."

Everyone became quiet. Ed had been sick, there was no denying that. Zach and Travis could still remember seeing Ed in hospital, pale as the sheets. How he got better was a mystery; he wasn't expected to make it out of the hospital alive!

At that moment, a head the size of a tennis ball poked out from Ed's coat pocket. It was made from burlap with multiple stitches where the material had torn over time with a few odd hairs remaining. The head moved about, looking at everyone with a mischievous grin.

"Hullo!" the head cried, in a high-pitched voice.

"I forgot you were in there," added Ed. He drew the figure out from his pocket. "Everybody, meet Little Dill."

Everyone could see as Little Dill hopped out from Ed's coat pocket that the doll was dressed in a fine suit of purple and a vest of lovely yellow.

"How cute." Alice commented, as she tried to reach for Little Dill.

"Don'ts t'ink abou' it lady!" the toy shrieked.

"Little Dill doesn't really trust strangers," informed Ed.

"Dat's right!" Little Dill squeaked. "For alls I know you peepers could bees holding us cap'ive."

Alice looked hurt after hearing these words.

"Don't worry," continued Ed. "You'll have lots of time to get to know him."

"What do you mean?" Travis asked.

"Oh, nothing." Ed shrugged as he walked to the fireplace and glanced into the grate. "I only planned to take you all with me when I go back."

"What?" cried everyone.

"Little Dill!" Ed ordered, ignoring the response. "Get me the call bell."

The little toy ran to the carpetbag and produced from it a bell, the kind you would see at a hotel desk. Ed took the bell and laid it on the top of the fireplace and pressed the little button on top. The chimney pipe rattled and out from its mouth came a burst of black and blue smoke that cleared to reveal an old wizard in strange garb.

He wore a blue velvet coat and trousers over a frilly shirt, red and gold waistcoat, and a long paisley cravat that seemed to fade in and out of different colours wrapped around the shirt collar, while a little silk cap that looked like it all belonged to a time centuries ago rested on his head. On his hands were multiple rings with strange ruins engraved into them and a broad chain that stretched from the middle button on the waistcoat like arms into the pockets. The wizard looked as ancient as his clothes, with a long and scraggly white beard that had a long wooden pipe protruding from it.

"'Bout time," said the old man with a shudder, as he wrung out the little cap and held it near the fire to dry. "It's an absolute deluge out there."

"Sorry, Bug-a-Boo," Ed replied. "I had to explain a few details."

"Excuses, more like," the old man said. "That'll be your downfall, your lack of awareness."

"Who is this guy?" questioned Travis.

"Oh! Where are my manners?" realized Ed. "Everyone, meet Professor Bug-a-Palooza-Pick-a-Low-Boo. Or you can just call him Professor Bug-a-Boo."

"What a fine to-do," Bug-a-Boo muttered impatiently, as he looked about his surroundings.

"What'd ye say?" asked Ed.

"Nothing." snapped Bug-a-Boo. "Now, are they coming or not?"

"That's not up to me," Ed replied, looking toward the others.

The three made no reply. They merely glanced at one another with an air of confusion.

"I haven't all night," fumed Bug-a-Boo, as he reached into his pocket and produced a silk bag. He then pulled out a handful of sand-like powder and threw it into the fireplace. The flames began to glow in multiple colours, emitting a glow much different to that of normal flame while multicoloured sparks danced about with each crackle and pop.

"I've opened the door," continued the sage. "They can make their decision whether to go in or not."

"And if we don't?" Zach inquired in a testing tone. He was not liking this old man's attitude and was equally not liking how the situation was going.

Bug-a-Boo, ignoring Zach's protest and everyone's confusion, disappeared in a puff of blue smoke.

Ed turned to the others with a kind glint in his eye. "I would really like to have you all come with me to this other world. If you come, you come. If you don't, you don't. I totally understand your suspicion." He then made a run for the fireplace and jumped headfirst into the opening. The flames flared for a brief second as it swallowed Ed and the young man disappeared.

Little Dill looked up at the others. "Are you comin'?" he squeaked.

Everyone gave a look of uncertainty, the kind that suggested: *I really want to go, but will it affect my schedule?*

"Can't you sees that he's alive?" Little Dill said, thinking he could coax them along. After a moment of no response, Little Dill jumped into the flames.

"I'm going in," Travis declared, and made a run for the fireplace. With a flash of flame, he was gone.

Only Alice and Zach were left. The flames were still giving off their glow, but they were beginning to shrink and the remaining ones were turning back to their familiar orange glow.

"Well?" asked Alice, with her head slightly tilted.

"Well, what?" quizzed Zach.

"Are you going in?"

To be quite honest, Zach was thinking he'd say *no*, but for a reason that could only be explained as "being in the spirit of the moment," or possibly indigestion, he said, "yes." Alice, in reaction to this, grabbed Zach by the hand and started to pull him along as she ran into the fire.

Chapter II
Through the Fireplace and What They Saw

Through the dark void Zach and Alice travelled. They felt as if they were in a sleeper hold, their heads swimming with a feeling of pressure, always growing until it was almost unbearable. As the pressure began to build, the blackness began to fade into different colours, wildly and randomly like flames in the fire were when Bug-a-boo threw the sand into the fireplace. Just as the pressure began to feel as if it was never going to end, they saw a flash of light and soon found themselves in a living room.

It wasn't a very fancy room. It was quaint and cozy with nice leather armchairs, couches and a television set that looked rather old. On the walls were paintings, ceramic plates, a wooden cuckoo clock, and an oil painting of an elder statesman that glared down at Zach and Alice from its home over the fireplace mantle.

Alice and Zach looked up and saw Ed and an old man. The old man was in salmon-coloured collarless shirt and grey trousers with a brown cardigan for warmth, and seemed to not be enjoying the fact that people were popping out of his chimney in the middle of the night.

"I trust you had a fun ride," said Ed.

"Why yes, I did," said Alice, with some smugness.

Zach didn't say anything, he was rather shaken by the journey from one fireplace to another.

Ed and the old man helped Alice and Zach up.

"Oh, dear," cried Ed. "My manners must have buggered off again. Everyone, this is George Hendrick McTrotter. He is a good friend of mine and I hope will be one of yours."

"Keep it down," warned George. "You'll wake up Emma."

"Sorry," Ed replied, curtly, and then resumed at a lower tone: "Anyways, shall we have some tea before heading out to my house?"

George brought out some china cups and saucers on a tray with a porcelain teapot, sugar bowl and a creamer.

"If I had known you were coming back sooner, I'd have bought some cakes at Sweetly's," George said, as he laid the tray on the coffee table.

"It's alright," Ed replied, "I can have those any other time. Plus, I hate being away for any longer than I need to be. By the way, has Ryan been keeping up with the place?"

"Aye, the boy's kept it up."

"Good." Ed replied.

"Who's Ryan?" Travis asked.

"That's my son," replied George, "he lives with yer friend here."

"This also reminds me," Ed added, "did he leave my motor here like I asked?"

"Aye, he did."

"Excellent," said Ed with relief. "Then when we are done our tea, we can set out."

"Where, are we exactly?" Zach inquired as he grabbed a cup and saucer.

"The United Crown Island of the Gallan-Gallet,[1]" Ed explained, "the cultural and political center of the Deltic[2] Empire."

"That it?" Zach quested, not satisfied with the answer.

"Well, what else do you want to know?" Ed replied. "If it's whether or not we are still in Canada, then the answer is *no*."

"So, what is this exactly then? Are you saying this is like Narnia or Middle Earth? Am I gonna get kidnapped by some faun? Or is some wizard going to give me a ring to drop in a volcano?"

---

[1] Pronounced Găll/Ăn/-/Găll/ĕt

[2] Pronounced Děll/Tĭck

Ed gave a confuddled look and put down his tea in a way that suggested he was about to get serious.

"You, Zacchaeus Dartmouth," Ed described, making sure to sound as clear and concise as possible, "are in another world. If you go outside this house, you will see houses and streetlamps, like in our world. The significant difference is that there are humans, talking animals, and other mystical creatures that will be walking those streets and among those street lamps. Do you think you can comprehend that?"

Zach didn't answer.

"Come now, Ed. That's rather rude of you." George commented. "He's probably confused with everything that is going on. I would be too, if I was hopscotched out of where I know into somewhere I didn't."

After everyone finished their tea, Ed led them out the front door, where they descended a few stairs to a driveway upon which two old cars sat. They were boxy and ancient looking. Ed then unlocked the door, and everyone piled in. After, Ed spent several minutes turning a crank on the front of the car, it rattled and groaned to life, then backed out and headed down the road.

"Where are we going?" investigated Zach, who was still not at all impressed with the setting.

"To my place, of course," Ed replied. "It's only a few miles up the road. We'll be there in only twenty minutes."

The car darted uphill with its engine rattling as it made the climb. When it reached the top, it rattled to the right and then it rattled straight down the road, only stopping at traffic lights. The streets were empty, save for the odd police constable making their rounds or a passing car or steam tractor bringing goods from outside of town. After going straight for a while, the car turned right and rolled down a street lined with houses until they approached a peaceful-looking cottage.

The house stood at the end of a lush green lawn with a grey stone path in the middle leading from the road to its small porch. A birch tree sat on one side of the path; the other side was a bed covered in dark soil that would have had wild flowers dwelling in the summertime. Ed drove the car into the driveway and led everyone to the front door.

"This is the place!" announced Ed, as he unlocked the door and led them inside.

The house looked wonderful. The walls were covered in paintings of both scenery and people. To their left was the living room, lovingly decorated with brown leather chairs, and at the far end was a massive set of shelves filled to the brim with books and a grand hearth for fires. On the right was a set of wooden stairs that led to the bedrooms. Across from them, at the other end of the hall, were two openings: the left one led to the kitchen and the other to a washroom, side door and stairs to the basement. As the three observed their friend's surroundings, the light scent of books and tea floated in the air.

"I don't think Ryan will mind if you guys take his bed for the night." Ed said, as he removed his overcoat and hat to reveal a brown tweed suit with a gold chain.

"For the night?" inquired Zach.

"Well, you can't leave after only just getting here," replied Ed. "I'll give you all the grand tour as we head upstairs. I trust you lot will be in need of some sleep."

The second floor was decorated much the same as the former, with portraits and paintings of scenery hanging on the walls. At the top of the stairs was the bathroom, which was floored with brown tile and wood cabinets for storing towels and the like. As the group turned left, they saw two doors along the left wall. The one closest to the stairs was Ed's study while the other was his bedroom. Straight ahead was another door that was Ryan's room while along the right was another door that was typically reserved for guests.

It was decided that Alice would have the bed in the spare room and Zach would have the couch in Ed's study, while Travis slept in Ryan's room. "It's only for one night." Ed assured as he showed them to their rooms. "Ryan usually doesn't get home until the morning anyway since he's the night watchman at the harbour, so there shouldn't be much of an issue."

That night, the three slipped into an uncomfortable sleep, unsure if they were only in a dream.

Chapter III
The Trip to Town

Zach awoke from a difficult sleep, the kind of sleep where you hope the events from the day before were nothing but a terrible dream. But in truth, they were very real. The couch that he slumbered on was obviously not meant for sleeping, or sitting for that matter. He studied the room as he pulled himself out of the makeshift bed.

The walls were covered with shelves, each filled with books, scrolls, and boxes. In one corner of the room, Zach noticed a small desk with a stack of paper and a large typewriter. He went over and studied it; the top sheet read: "An insightful study of Grogs in the Deadlands." Zach placed the slice of paper back on the stack.

Nonsense, he thought, *Grogs...what the hell is that! The Deadlands seemed to be some region that was lazily named.* All these things seemed to him to be nothing more than made-up nonsense.

Zach opened the bedroom door. He heard the sound of laughter and the smell of tea and cooking coming from downstairs. As he walked down the hall and the stairs, Zach studied the paintings that decorated the walls. When he reached the kitchen, Zach saw that everyone was sitting around a table in the middle of breakfast.

Ed sat in a beige cardigan over some red-striped pajamas with Travis and Alice on either side of him. Next to Alice sat a young man with a sleepy look to him who appeared to be in his twenties, dressed in navy-blue jacket and trousers and a white shirt with a black tie that was loosened for comfort. A navy-blue cap rested lazily on his head of auburn hair, with its black brim brass label reflecting the kitchen light.

"...and so there I was, running from a six-foot talking bee when—Oh, Zach!" cried Ed, as he tapped a boiled egg with a spoon. "Glad to see you're up. This is Ryan, George's son."

Zach nodded hello and took an uneasy seat next to Travis. The table was littered with toast, eggs, plates, cups, and a large bellied teapot steaming with tea; Zach selected a bit of each and joined the others in the meal.

"I've been telling one of my travel stories," Ed explained as he shook some salt onto the egg.

"I see," Zach replied, with a tone suggesting that he was still not quite comfortable with the situation.

There soon came a moment of uncomfortable silence.

"I was hoping," added Ed, wanting to break the silence as he carefully scooped the exposed white top of his egg, "that we could maybe make a trip to the older district of Newtown, if it is at all possible."

"Older district?" puzzled Travis.

Before Ed could answer, the doorbell rang. "I'll get it!" Ryan said, as he got up from the table.

"It's just the central area of town," Ed explained. "There are some lovely shops and I need to make some enquiries."

"Whatever happened to that little toy from last night?" Alice asked. She had a point; Little Dill had disappeared after they arrived at George's house.

"Here I ams!" cried a familiar voice.

Everyone looked. On the windowsill was Little Dill, dressed in his purple coattails. Next to him was another doll, a little taller than Little Dill. The other doll was dressed in a flashy suit.

"Hullo, Gary, haven't seen you in these parts for a while," greeted Ed.

"I've been traveling around selling yards," the doll replied.

"Yards?" asked Zach.

"Yeah," replied Ed. "Gary and Little Dill sell yards."

"They're three feet of fun!" cried Little Dill, with excitement.

There came a sigh in response to this poor pun.

"Oh!" cried Ed. "Where have my manners gone again? Everyone, this is Gary."

Gary gave a polite bow. After he and Little Dill made their excuses, they set out the window to continue with whatever work they had to do.

Ryan soon returned with what looked like a box wrapped in brown paper. "The starchier came by with your collars," he said, and tossed the box on the counter.

Soon the ritual of breakfast was over, and Ed changed into a grey suit and a black tie with a ruby stud on it. The others had nothing to change into and had to go out in the same clothes they had warn the night before.

Ed led the group down the path to the sidewalk where they all climbed into the car. The street looked peaceful in the autumn sun as the car prattled away, passing other little houses along the way.

The Older District was located not far from the downtown area. A large, red-bricked building that Ed called "The Market House" marked its location. Large grey stone walls that branched from the Market House surrounded the district, which was clearly dated from days past. The streets and roads were built in a time when it was uncommon for vehicles, whether draft animal- or motor-powered, to enter the town limits during the day, so many visitors would park their cars in a yard nearby and walk into the district.

Upon arriving, the group were led to an old building with a sign with odd ruins. "Cheswick Tailors!" Ed announced as they approached.

The store front of Cheswick's while large seemed rather cramped. Readymade suits and shelves of shirts lined the walls, while an unnecessarily large desk bordered part of the floor with the front part having multiple stands carrying shirts, collars, and silk ties. Ed walked up to the desk and rapped upon it. From a small door behind the desk emerged a haggard man and his wife.

Must be that Cheswick fellow, Zach thought.

"What would you be likin'?" the Mr. Cheswick inquired in a crusted manner and straightened up, making his back crackle rather loudly.

"Just needin' some new cloths for some gents and a young lady," Ed replied and gestured to the three.

Mr. Cheswick eyed Zach and Travis up and down. "Kids today," he muttered, "looking sloppier and sloppier every year."

The tailor searched among his many ready-made clothes for something that met their style, while Mrs. Cheswick helped Alice find something appealing. In the meantime, Ed had run across the street to send out some telegrams from the post office. The parcels from the shop were loaded onto a handcart, which a porter was hired to pull. As they walked, they came across a shop with a well-kept sign that Ed read to them as "Jelly's Fine Meats and Delicatessen."

It was not busy in the shop; at the front, three men were arguing—two of them in front of the counter and one behind. One of the men in front of the counter was George from the night before—dressed in a suit and worn bowler hat this time—and the other was in a purple vest with a black top hat and had an impressively thick moustache that met with his sideburns to create a handlebar effect. The man behind the counter was dressed in a shirt and tie with a crisp white smock, which made his reddened frustrated face stand out.

"I am telling you, it's your turn to pay for pints," snapped George and tapped on the counter for emphasis.

"And I'm telling you, it's yours," replied the man behind the counter.

"I paid for them last week," put in the man in the purple vest. "It's always your turn after me, so stop being a miser."

"George paid last time," the smocked man replied, clearly seeming to grasp at any tread he could to get out of his obligation. "I remember because Lordham went purple when he saw you pulling out your cheque book. 'No merchant likes it when you use cheques,' my da' always said, 'it tells them that your skint.'"

"Oh, bolt your da' and his quips," George replied. "That was just to guarantee to Lordham that he got his copper. Tha' was two weeks ago, anyways."

"What's all this?" inquired Ed.

"Jelly here is refusing to pay for pints tonight," explained George, pointing at the man in the smock with his thumb.

"It happens every week it's his turn," added the man in the vest, with a sigh.

Ed turned to his friends. "Everyone," he said, "this,"—pointing to the man in the vest— "is Jackson Oakwood, and"—pointing to the man in the smock— "this is Theodorus Jelly, everyone calls him Teddy."

"You can call me Pumpkin Stone," added the man in the vest (who we shall refer to as Pumpkin Stone for the remainder of the story).

"There is always a more appropriate way of solving this," added Ed.

"And what would that be?" quipped Jelly.

"A game of Pumpernickel, obviously."

"Excellent plan," added George, "but I can't play 'cause of my leg." He pointed to the one in question, and leaned on his cane to emphasise his feebleness.

"Then we'll have Alice, Zach and Travis join in and you can observe from the side."

"But can they play?" Pumpkin Stone asked.

"I'm sure they can learn quick," George replied confidently. "Besides, we haven't much of a choice at this juncture."

Alice, Zach and Travis just watched. The name of the game was strange enough, and they were actually going to play it!

"Well," considered Jelly, "it has been a long time since I've played a round of Pumpernickel. I suppose a game would easily resolve the issue."

"Right." agreed George. "Suppose we meet at Mornhide Common in half an hour?"

"I suppose I could manage that." Jelly replied and checked his watch. "I'll need to arrange for Bokem to come in but that should be hard. I know he wants the hours."

On the drive to the field, Ed tried his best to explain the game.

"It's really easy. All we need are a few bats, two poles and a ball. The whole point of the game is to try and get the ball to hit your opponent's pole and get the most points, or a "tri," as it's called in the game."

"Sounds easy enough." Travis agreed.

"Also, I'd recommend watching for Teddy." Ed went as the car rounded a bend. "He tends to get a bit competitive when it comes to pumpernickel, especially when pints are on the line."

The car turned onto the embankment of a steep hill and charged upward, the car growling crossly as it made the assent and bouncing about on the uneven terrain. At the peak of the hill sat some swings and a slide at one end, and a flat pasture planted with two poles on the other. George and Pumpkin Stone walked up the hill with a trunk held between them. Once at the top they dumped out the contents: a few short bats and a ball made of rubber bands.

"What happed to the ball I got you last Long Night Festival?" Pumpkin Stone asked.

"Mrs. Beacon's dog ran off with it," George explained. "Ugly little thing buried it somewhere along the back alley, but I haven't the time to look."

"Did you ever think to make her buy you a replacement?" Pumpkin Stone proposed casually. "They aren't that expensive; only ten gil at Gogog and Sons."

"I've tried that." George rebuked. "The hag won't part with even a gil if it means she's in the wrong. Not to mention she denies any responsibility, despite leaving that putrid dog unattended to run the streets all the time."

"Then sue." Pumpkin Stone suggested. "You can charge 'er for theft and careless watch."

"That wouldn't work at all." George replied.

"And why not?"

"It isn't financially reasonable. A proper pumpernickel ball is about a crown at most."

"Aye, but the one I got you was a Red Line series. Was a crown and a half."

"Alright, a crown and a half. That still won't qualify for a suit in the lower courts. Wait! You bought me a pumpernickel ball for a crown and a half?"

"Never mind about that." Pumpkin Stone replied. "Just get to the point."

"Oh alright. Even if we did get through, Weston Belmont is still deputy justice of the Middle Tashford circuit. Considering his views on Emma and I 'cause of Ryan's run-ins with the law when he was a lad, I wouldn't be surprised if he ruled against us. Also, the Office of Lord Chancellor just raised the legal fee in the lower courts another ten sovereign. All in all, it's not even worth the effort."

Pumpkin Stone just sighed. He had known George for just over seventy years. Since they were schoolboys at Montford Hall and later Lord Buchannan Collegiate, Pumpkin Stone and George had stood side by side in any challenge that faced them. When George went off to serve in the Deltic army during the Emo War in '58 and years later when he had his stroke in the autumn of '88, Pumpkin Stone worked to make sure that Emma was taken care of when George wasn't able. It was from all these experiences that Pumpkin Stone had learned a very important lesson: George Hendrik McTrotter could be a stubborn bastard. Once George had made up his mind on something, it was near impossible to make him see otherwise.

"What's he on about?" Travis asked.

"About what?" asked Ed.

"Crowns and sovereigns."

"Deltic currency," Ed explained. "Rather odd really. It's made up of gils, sovereigns, and crowns. I think it's twelve gil to a sovereign, and twenty sovereigns to a crown."

"Sound's a bit hard to keep track."

"It's rather finicky, I still have problems remembering it all sometimes when I go to the shops. Once I went to the butchers for some mutton. The butcher charged five gil a pound and I bought ten. So, five times ten is fifty. Then you have to divvy it all up so that's fifty divided by twelve… so four sovereign and sixteen gil, or four and sixteen. Anyway, I got so confused that I panicked and accidentally gave the butcher a twenty-crown note. The look on his face was priceless."

There came a sudden "toot-toot," and up the embankment came an old lorry driven by Teddy. He had abandoned his smock for a checked coat and a cloth cap.

"Right," he said. "Who's all playing?"

"Since George is useless without his cane," said Pumpkin Stone, "he's going to keep score and I'll play in his place."

"If he's so feeble-legged," Teddy protested (he always protested when George excused himself from anything strenuous), "How the blue devil did you get that trunk up the hill?"

"We loaded it in Ed's motor." Pumpkin Stone rebuked, knowing that if he sounded cross enough, Teddy would back down.

Teddy said no more on the matter, he gestured Ed over to where he and Pumpkin Stone were standing. "Do your friends know how to play?" he asked in a low whisper, sounding as if they were talking about something scandalous.

"Oh, of course," Ed replied, speaking in a normal tone. "I even explained the whole thing to them, to be safe."

Teddy did not seem satisfied, but whether he liked it or not, Alice, Zach and Travis were the only players they had. He knew this game would be his only way to weasel out of paying for drinks. With an annoyed sigh, Teddy replied, "Ball, set, and match." Teddy then turned to Travis and called: "You're wit' me."

"I'll go on Pumpkin Stone's team," called Ed.

Zach was shunted to Teddy's team and Alice to Pumpkin Stone's. George threw the old ball of rubber bands into the air and then walked over to sit on the trunk, where he lit his pipe and watched the game. George cried: "First team to thirty wins!"

Ed struck the ball with this bat. It flew in the air and was struck in turn by Pumpkin Stone, and it bounced off the pole on one end.

"Three points!" called George and wrote it onto a scrap of paper.

The ball was now in the air, Alice caught it and began to run.

"Foul!" yelled George, and he scratched the three points out.

"You can't grab the ball and run," explained Ed. "You can only catch it and throw to another person on your team or strike it with the bat."

"I wish you'd told me that sooner," Alice grumbled.

The game went on uneventfully for the rest of the time. At least, that was the case until Travis ruined Teddy's chance of evading his role as payer. Teddy was close to winning the game. They had twenty-seven points to Pumpkin Stone's eighteen. One more tri and Teddy would win.

The ball flew in the air toward Travis. He didn't know what to do. He closed his eyes tightly and swatted his bat. The ball flew toward his right and kept going. Then: "Crash!" Right into a window of a house at the far end.

"Not again," sighed Pumpkin Stone, and buried his face in his hands.

The group quickly tossed what remained of the equipment into the trunk, returned it to the back of Teddy's lorry and drove off as fast as possible. No one knows what happened after the escape, but George swears that sometime later Mrs. Beacon came to his house to return the ball her dog had taken.

The Boar's Head was built in 1890 by the brewery Gilbert and Co. on the corner of Rambole Street and Tashford Road. If you were to ever walk into the pub, you would notice that it was divided into two parts. One side—the original part of the pub when it was first constructed—held the bar, kitchen entrance and a few dartboards, while the other side— added on in 1960—contained tables, chairs, and a few benches for dominos. Over the years it had become a second home for those returning from the lumber mill on Loot Hill, the dock workers who worked at the harbour near the railway station on the Tashford River, and the white collared teachers who had finished their long days of teaching bratty children at Broad Head Grammar School or hormonal teenagers at Lord Buchannan Collegiate. It wasn't uncommon to see elves from the Eastern territory of the island or dwarven merchants stopping in for a few moments rest before traveling further along the Tashford.

The septet walked in and were greeted by a burly man with thick sideburns dressed in a herring bone shirt and starched collar, tweed vest, matching trousers, and a well-worn black tie. "Goo' eve'in'," he called from behind the bar, in a deep, bold voice.

"Hullo, Lordham," cried Ed, as he and the rest of the company took a few tables.

Lordham walked over to them, pointing at each of the familiars and naming their usual drinks: George— "Local ale," Pumpkin Stone— "local ale," Teddy— "soda and gin," and Ed— "milk stout." Lordham then turned to Alice, Zach and Travis and asked for their orders.

"I don't drink," said Zach, politely.

"Doesn't mattah teh me, lad," was the reply. "Ah can get you a syrup an' soda instead."

"You'll like it," Ed whispered. "Tastes like lime and Coke."

Alice and Travis placed their orders as well, rum and soda and ale respectively. Lordham disappeared for what seemed like a brief moment, only to return with a tray of various drinks and a plate of complementary meat pies.

There they were, George, Pumpkin Stone, Teddy, Ed, Alice, Zach and Travis, sitting comfortably, each sipping their drinks away. It was peaceful for Ed, very peaceful. His eyes began silently tearing up as he drank his milk stout. It occurred to him then that they would go home soon. Back to their daily lives, and Ed would be left to fret away on another journey of his own. They may never meet again, the whole lot spreading out to the point where Ed would never find them.

Ed's train of thought was broken by Travis: "What up, bro?" he said.

"Nothing," Ed replied, "just thinking."

"Don't do too much of that, you'll hurt yourself."

Ed smirked. "I was only thinking, what'll happen once this is over? You guys will be off and living your lives again. I'll just sit here and try to make the most of my new life."

"We know you're alive now," Travis assured his friend. "I mean, there should be a way for us to visit you any time we wanted."

"Maybe. Bug-a-Boo mentioned to me once that there is more than one way to travel among worlds. In fact, the one we took is one of but a few that I am aware of."

Ed was about to say more but he was interrupted by George. "Looks like Bell Coop, Sanford Jenkins, and Daffy Tucker made it in from the mill."

Alice, Zach and Travis looked over see a trio of youngish men in collarless shirts, worn coats and caps gathered about the bar.

"Three more pints, Lordy." Daffy ordered as he placed a note on the bar counter.

Lordham fulfilled request with an air of annoyance, he even threw the change back at Daffy, hoping that would scare the young miller away. The three men started singing and dancing about the pub room with no regard for anyone hoping for a quiet evening drink. The boisterous racket made it hard for Ed and company, or even anyone else in the pub, to carry a conversation.

> Takin' a walk do'n to the shop
> At farmer's wages, you won' fin' much!
> Hidey ho! Ho-dee hay!
> Takin' a trip on Market Day!
>
> Find a fa' hog! Six crown each.
> Fin' 'em cheap at the auction seat.
> Hidey ho! Ho-dee hay!
> Nah mu' luck on a Market Day!
>
> Meet a nice girl at the pub.
> The nicer kind tha'll make no fuss.
> Hidey ho! Ho-dee hay!
> Mu' more luck than a' Market Day!

Just as the trio finished their shanty, Sanford lost balance and bumped into a large beefy fellow in a tweed jacket who was none to pleased when the collision made him spill his draught of beer.

"What in the name of a cat's maw are ye doin'?" the beefy fellow fumed as he turned around.

"Sorry Chuck," Sanford replied. "Di'n't see ye there."

"Listen here you, mango maggot," Chuck flounced, "I've 'ad to spend all day running that steam cutter and the noise 'as lef' a ringin' in me ear. Ah came in 'er to have a sup in peace. No' to lis'en to yer ear bleedin' singin'."

"Looks like you could stan' to cut back on a few pints," Sanford replied, having no sympathy for Chuck.

Chuck's face went red with rage and swung at Sanford, but the latter ducked in time only for Chuck to lose balance and run into a few other labourers. What followed was a mess of workmen throwing fists and beer glasses.

"What going on?" asked Alice, who was confused by the commotion.

"Nothing, dear. Just a normal pub fight on a Market Day," George explained, as he smashed a bottle over a man's head without looking.

Near the kitchen entrance, Lordham seemed to be signaling them.

"Now's our cue to leave, lads," called Pumpkin Stone, as he tucked a few meat pies in his coat pocket.

The group followed Lordham through the kitchen to the lounge room in the back.

"We've 'ad fights in 'ere before," said Lordham, as he poured some coffee into a mug, "but this 'un 'as teh beat tha' one incident when we went to the Imperial Inn as lads."

"Yes!" Pumpkin Stone agreed as a wave of nostalgia hit him, making the gears in his mind begin to whirl. "I remember… it was George, me, an' Empire Jones who got there early. I don't remember Teddy bein' there, but… I know you were late, Lordham."

"Aye," Lordham agreed. "My da' decided that the was the night we needed to count the barrels for the month. I personally think he didn't want me to go the Imperial. Isa and I would never like our Jaco going there an' he's all grown and on his own."

"If he knew what went on that night between us and 'Clop Mouth' Jenkins, Weston Belmont, and Danny 'Rubber Tongue' Faythe, I think he would have locked you up in stern tighter than what Constable Goy did."

George started laughing. "I thought my da' was going to kill me when he picked us up from the police station. All he would say on the way home was: 'Do that again and you're off to St. Tyrone's.'"

"I've said it before, an' I'll say it again," Pumpkin said as he took another swig of ale, "I have no regrets taking a swing ol' Clop Mouth. Maybe it'll teach him to mind his manners around the young women."

"Didn't you break your hand punching Clop?"

"Yup. Still throbs when the rain falls, too.

While the old men talked of their youthful escapades, Ed explained the situation. Whenever a fight would break out on Market Day's evening, Lordham and the others would hide out in the back room until it ended, or the police finally showed up to break it up.

Ed took Alice, Zach and Travis back to his house. When they arrived, Ryan was just leaving for his shift at work. Before departing, Ryan told Ed that a letter had arrived for him in the evening mail. Ed glanced at the address and placed it with the other envelopes.

"I'll be back," Ed said, bluntly. He hurried up the stairs and shut his office door behind him.

With Ed gone, Zach spoke: "Something isn't right. Am I the only one who thinks…well, you know?"

"What?" Alice asked.

"Ed…he seems different."

"You sound surprised," said a voice from nowhere.

The three looked over to the empty living room. Suddenly, with the strike of a match and the hazy smoke from a pipe, Bug-a-Boo appeared in one of the leather chairs.

"How'd you get in here?" Travis inquired.

"It is well within my abilities to be anywhere, anytime," the wizard explained. "Did it ever occur to you why he wanted to have you lot here?"

No one said a word.

"He's trying to say goodbye."

"But Ed told me there was more than one way to come here," Travis projected.

"He is quite right," Bug-a-boo countered, "but as true as it may be, giving someone the power to cross worlds is very dangerous. That's why I opened the portal myself. I can't just trust anyone else with it, they may use it for corrupt reasons. When I had let Edward cross between worlds, I realized he would eventually have to choose where he would want to dwell. That is why I brought him here when he was ill, to give him a new start once he was in better health. He doesn't understand the gravity of the situation. I was able to make him agree to only have you lot come once. Once you were all done saying your good-byes, however long that may be, Edward is to notify me so that I can reopen the portal and allow you three to go home."

"That's why he made the list."

"Indeed."

"If Ed is saying goodbye, why does he seem to be so happy about it?" Travis snapped.

"Just because a man acts happy doesn't mean he really is, nor does it mean he's not trying to say goodbye."

At that moment, Ed came down the stairs. "Bug-a-Boo," he said. "I wasn't expecting you here. What's up?"

"Nothing, I only came to pass a message on to you." The wizard replied, wearily. "Kina wants you to stop by his house in the morning. He sent some particulars for you to look at for when you see him. He didn't say what it was about, only that it was of the utmost importance."

"I know," Ed replied politely, "I was actually just glancing them over in the office."

"Very good," Bug-a-boo replied curtly and with a few puffs of his pipe, the wizard faded from his audience.

Chapter IV
Reports From Apothem

By the light of an old lamp, Ed sat at his writing desk in his pajamas and dressing gown studying the dossier Kina had sent about a city in a in the Grand Duchy of the Fineylands[3] called Apothem. The reports from inside the city told of a mysterious purple cloud rolling into the area and looming over it for several days, before finally descending upon Apothem. The second set came from one of the traveling outposts of the Order of the Four Keepers. They claimed that after the cloud ascended from Apothem, the entire population had vanished without a trace.

---

[3] Pronounced Fin/ē/lands

Praep 23, 2006 AR[4]

At 800 hours on 10 Praep, 2006, my team and I received a wireless message from Order headquarters of a strange anomaly that had appeared over the city of Apothem, a major city in the nation of the Grand Dutchy of the Fineylands. The cloud had appeared five to six days prior and had shown no signs of moving. It was also reported that Lake Twinmar[6], a major water source for the city, had frozen over in the wake of the cloud's arrival.

After conferring with my team, it was decided to travel to Apothem at once to see if we could be of any assistance. Due to being along the southern border of the Deadlands, the estimated time to reach the city was three days. During this journey south, we continued to maintain contact with Apothem headquarters for any possible updates that may have occurred.

---

[4] Author's note: When the Melkian calendar was instituted, the chroniclers divided history into two parts to differentiate between before the creation of the calendar and after: Before Reckoning—BR—and After Reckoning—AR.

[5] Pronounced Twin/M/air

On the second day of our journey, we had received correspondence that the cloud had started to descend. Through out the day, I received updates of the cloud's movements. There was an attempt to warn the Finian government of the situation but no reply was received.

Upon the arriving in Apothem, the following day, we were surprised to find the entire city appeared intact. From outside the city walls, there seemed no sign of anything having happened.

Upon entering Apothem, we found that there was no sign of life within...

Further reports confirmed the findings of the first group of no life being found after the cloud landed. Photographs showed whole buildings standing tall and stoic like silent sentinels while the rest of the area seemed frozen in time with everything left as it was just before the rapture.

Once finished reading, Ed began to leaf through the dossier again, trying to look for common threads. The purple cloud seemed oddly familiar. Ed needed to consult his book of Deltic Myths, but there was one problem: the shelf that the book rested on loomed over Zach, who was fast asleep on the couch.

Ed looked about him. Conveniently nearby was a wooden ladder that Ed had brought in to replace the current one leading to the loft. Silently, Ed leaned it against the shelf and began to climb. As Ed went up, the shelf groaned from the weight. Nervously, Ed reached for the book, inching cautiously with each step.

Zach rolled over. The couch jerked forward and bumped the ladder. Ed gripped the sides tightly as he waited for the shuddering to stop. When it did, Ed continued his mission.

As soon as the book was in Ed's hands, down went the shelf and its contents, including Ed and the book, right on top of Zach and the couch.

I wish I could say it was a harmless incident, but the fact that a penknife nearly stabbed Zach in the shoulder and that Zach chased Ed out of the room with it would only prove that I was lying. Ed, flustered, retreated to the kitchen to read his book while waiting for everyone else to wake up, leaving Zach to dig through the mountain of books and papers for a comfortable place to sleep.

The morning routine was the same as before, except this time everyone had new clothes to wear from the trip to the tailors. Ed sported a dark three-piece with a wing collar and a silver tie, while Travis and Zach wore collarless shirts and grey trousers and Alice a blue dress.

"I have some business to attend to this morning," Ed explained over breakfast. "My Order's director, Dr. Abraham Kina, needs to speak with me about the particulars that I received last night."

"What's it about?" Travis asked through a mouthful of toast.

"Nothing serious," Ed replied innocently

Zach glared, secretly not believing Ed's assurance.

Kina's house was a red brick building near the Old District. The car rolled to a halt near the curb in front of the house and Ed led the crew to the front door where a young woman, in what looked like her good dress, greeted them.

"Morning Katherine!" Ed called. "Is Dr. Kina in?"

"He's in his office," was the cheery reply.

Ed went ahead up the stairs, leaving the others to be entertained by Katherine Kina.

Dr. Abraham Kina was ancient-looking with a bushy greying beard that looked well overdue for shaving. Dressed in a white shirt, black trousers, grey tie, and blue cardigan, he sat at his desk studying copies of the same reports that were sent to Ed.

"I trust you read the reports," he said, getting right to business.

"I did."

Kina opened a drawer and produced a reel of black tape. "This is a recording from one of the Order's outposts in Apothem. It starts just as the cloud is spotted over the city and goes until the cloud lands." Kina put the tape on a player with a hand crank. As soon as the handle was turned, this is what they heard: "This is Thaddeus Gallows of the Order of the Four

Keepers. Right now, there is a plume of purple smoke or something coming this way. No one knows what it is or if it's from a chemical accident or something. It seems to be coming down now. Quite quick dropping too! It's real thick. OH! What's that!?"

And then another voice: "Manookoo!"[6]

Ed shuddered. The voice at the end sounded hoarse, angry and lustful, all in one word. The word "Manookoo" seemed odd, almost familiar. He scribbled the name down on a piece of paper.

"In a week's time," explained Kina, "the Order will be presenting its findings before Parliament when both halls meet. This will be their final meeting before the sessional recess. Our sources are tracking the cloud and it is heading here. The Gallan-Gallet will not be able to fight back unless we can be properly prepared. Ed, I want you to write a report and present it before Parliament."

"In a week?" asked Ed, with some hesitation.

"Yes. Time is of the essence and our Mr. Bloom ensures us Her Majesty would eagerly agree with our proposal if we present the matter to her."

"I'll have to look into it some more first. That Manookoo bit seemed familiar."

"I would recommend seeing George McTrotter about it," Kina said, with finality. "He's more educated

---

[6] Pronounced Man/oo/Koo

in old languages and myth, I'm sure he'll be able to help you get to the bottom of it."

After this, Ed left. The other three had to run to keep up with Ed as he marched back to the car.

Ed was oddly quiet as he drove out to George's house. Zach tried to press him for what was going on, but Ed remained quiet. Alice and Travis also thought he was acting peculiar. Every now and again, Ed would begin muttering to himself. It was unnerving.

The car rolled to a halt in front of some familiar townhouses. George's wife, Emma McTrotter, was in her gardening clothes and tending to the flowerbed. While George was working on an old car on the driveway.

"Blasted thing," George cursed. "Of all the days to give out on me and after I had 'er refuelled with petrol too! Emma: if your sister asks to borrow our motor again, the answer is no. That horrid woman must've been driving' rough on Thrip Way again. No wonder, too! The belt's snapped!"

Emma seemed to ignore the torrent of cursing that spewed from her husband. She turned to see what George was doing now and caught the sight of Ed and company at the bottom of the drive.

"Hullo Ed!" Emma declared. "Lemon, get yourself from out of there and watch your language. We've company."

"Hulloa!" Ed called as he Alice, Travis, and Zach all walked up the drive.

"Hullo," called George as he pulled himself out from inside the car and wiped his hands with a rag as he made his way down the drive to meet Emma and the others. "My, you looked smart today. Attend church?"

"No," Ed replied, "I just came from Kina's for some order business. Do you know anything about something called *Manookoo*?"

"Sounds Zeltic,"[7] was the reply. "I believe I have something in the study about that. Come along, the two of us should be able to make short work of it."

While Ed followed George into the house, Emma spoke with Zach, Travis and Alice.

"'Tis a pity we didn't get to meet a few nights ago," Emma said graciously as she whipped dirt off her hands. "Lemon told me you three were quite 'spectful when you popped through our chimney."

"Lemon?" Alice asked confusedly.

"Oh, my apologies dearie," Emma replied. "Tha's jus' my pet name for George."

"How long have you known Ed?" Zach inquired, wanting to cut to the chase.

"Abou' few years nah." Emma explained after a minute to ponder. "Ol' Bug-a-boo brought him over one evenin' fer tea. Poor fellow looked pale as a sheet and thin as one too when Lemon an' I me' him."

"So, he was here around the time he got sick," Zach concluded.

---

[7] Pronounced Zĕl/Tĭck

"Yes." Emma replied. "He started gettin' weaker when he decided to settle up in Newtown. Doc Hamilton took good care of him, though. Edward was right as the Tashford in Spring by the time his affairs were in order."

Zach's fist clenched in frustration. Though, he was able to hide it, Zach felt offended that Ed had decided to abandon everyone for this world. Was he mad at George and Emma? *No. It wasn't their fault Ed decided to move here*, Zach thought to himself. *They seem like nice enough people, like they want to be everyone's grandparent.*

Just then George and Ed returned from inside the house with a collection of various thick books under their arms.

"These," George explained as he and Ed stepped out the door, "should be of some help. However, to my knowledge Manookoo was the name of a cult in Zeltic myth. They pop up all the time in the Lomassmay[8] epics. It's hard for me to remember exactly, but the translations by William Tristian plus these commentaries by Delany Longman should do the trick. Fantastic reads in their own right."

"Thank you," Ed said gratefully as he accepted the tomes. "I wish we could stay longer but time and Kina wait for no man."

"Do come back," Emma insisted as everyone loaded into the car. "It would be nice to have you all for the Festival of the Long Night, or even for the Equinox Festival."

---

[8] Pronounced Lō/Măss/Māy.

Once at home, Ed shut himself in his office, forgetting that his friends were there, and set straight to work examining books and writing his report for the Order. Zach, Alice and Travis sat in the living room, listening to the loud clattering of a typewriter from the office above.

Zach became more frustrated and impatient. He stormed up to the office before Travis or Alice could stop him.

The office door shot open with a bang against the wall. Zach wasted no time letting out his annoyance. He found Ed huddled over one of the books intensely examining a passage through a pair of gold-rimmed glasses, his collar unclasped and tie loosened.

"I've had it!" Zach snapped.

"Had what?" Ed asked, ignorant of what was going on and didn't even look up from his work. "Did it taste any good?"

"I've just had it." Zach cried bitterly. "I've had enough of your arrogant attitude. It seems as if ever since you brought us here you've been showing off, and I'm sick of it!"

"I brought you guys here to show you a good time." Ed rebuked, finally looking at Zach. "I wanted to show you that I am alive and well and that everything would be fine. If-if you have an issue with my generosity-"

"Generosity? You just brought us here to show off and then leave us. It's just typical of you. You show up and then go off on your own adventure, ignoring everyone else in the process."

Ed looked gravely at Zach; his reading glasses perched toward the end of his nose. "Look," he said, finally. "I'm not trying to show off. I was never expecting to have this work thrown upon me. The only upside to this is that I can take you guys to Bathill.[9] Zach, what am I supposed to do? I want you guys here, but I have my duty to the Order and the Empire to uphold."

"Then ask us to help," Zach shot back emphatically. "You would have better luck."

Ed had to agree to this. Like it or not, it had been nearly two hours and he still had little information to go on. It wasn't long until all four were scattered about the room. Books and paper covered in notes littered the floor. Ed managed to find some books written in a calligraphy familiar to his friends that Ed could only call *Britannic*. It took a while weeding through these ancient tomes of the Zeltics, Deltics, tales of Lomassmay the Warrior, St. Oliver and the Golden Flute, and the many other tales that floated through these faerie lands. As dusk began to settle on the sleepy house, Ed and company made their way to the kitchen for a modest supper of sandwiches.

"Not much luck today," Travis said sleepily.

"For now, I guess," Ed replied. "I like to think that we made some headway."

---

[9] Pronounced Bath/ill

"You seem pretty optimistic," Alice noted.

"Well," Ed went on, "It's not so much a question of if the information exists, more where is it hiding."

The next morning, after breakfast, everyone set back to work reading. Little Dill joined them, but only ended up amusing himself by balancing one of Ed's fountain pens on his nose.

It was about noon when Alice jumped up excitedly.

"I've found it!" she proclaimed and threw an open book at Ed.

"Easy!" Ed warned. "These books are antique."

"But look!" Alice cried. "It's what we've been looking for!"

Looking down upon then page, Ed read aloud the following:

"In the days of the titans, a great war arose between them and the people of the faerie. Night and day, every living thing battled amongst one another. They called these days the Black Out for even the stars were too frightened to see the bloodshed that beset the land.

"There lived in a certain place a certain people in those days who worshiped Manoo[10], the bastard son of Horcus.[11] These people called themselves Manookoo for they believed to be the people of Manoo and sacrificed all those who wronged them in these black days.

---

[10] Pronounced Man/oo

[11] Pronounced H/or/cuz

"When Horcus learned of their trespass, his anger waxed hot. He demanded retribution for these wrong doing or would damn them for practicing human sacrifice. The Manookoo refused and Horcus became evermore infuriated.

"'With the power that I possess!' Horcus declared. 'I cast thee unto a rock!'

"Upon this rock they called Spyrus[12], for it traverse in many ways. Upon learning of these things, Manoo approached his father to parlay.

"'Dear father, why must thee punish these people so?' the young god asked.

"'My dear son,' Horcus replied, 'surely you forget the killing of life is a transgress against all of us. They refuseth to repent and thus must be punished in all my power.'

"'But father,' Manoo protested, 'shouldst not all life be therefore punished. Dost not the lion kill for its prey as the warrior kills to save a young maid.'

"Horcus was at a loss for words. In this loss, he became blinded in rage and he casted his bastard upon that rock known as Spyruss.

"By Kinmount's might and frosted tools, the rock was fashioned even more. The soul of the young god's life as its foundation for Manoo was the foundation of the Manookoo. In the shroud of purple, they will for

---

[12] Pronounced Spy/r/us

ever more wander these lands, with only the souls of the damned to quench his hunger."

Ed's face lit up upon finishing the passage. "This is it!" he declared as he slammed the book shut, instantly realizing he forgot to note the page.

It took the better part of the day for Ed, Alice, Zach and Travis to compile their notes. They then took turns dictating the report to Little Dill, who danced on the keys of Ed's typewriter to transcribe it all. When the job was done, they had a report of fifteen pages.

The next morning, Mr. Kina paid a visit. Under Ed's insistence, everyone had to be dressed in formal attire when the director of the Order of the Four Keepers arrived. The elderly professor arrived in a grey suit with a wool top coat and wide brimmed hat for warmth.

"Good morning," Kina greeted in a friendly but professional manner. "I trust the report is ready."

"It most certainly is." Ed replied and led the professor into the living room where the report sat on the coffee table near one of the couches.

"It looks quite long." Kina said as examined the stack of paper from afar.

"There was quite a bit of information and research to-uh…put together."

"I see." Kina replied with a slight sigh, though it was hard to tell whether or not it was in disappointment. "I am not to be disturbed while I read this," he said at last.

"Of course," Ed replied.

While Dr. Kina was left in the living room to read the report, Ed and the others sat in the kitchen with a pot of tea between them. Ed looked exceedingly nervous, he never did like the waiting period between giving a person a draft to read and their response, his hands shook as he tried to lift his teacup. Everyone else was quiet except Little Dill, who slurped his tea with great gusto.

"Shush!" Ed ordered to the small doll.

"Will you relax?" Zach snapped. "You're over reacting."

"I'm most certainly not." Ed flounced as he picked up his cup and saucer, which clattered loudly as his hands shook.

It wasn't long before Kina joined them in the kitchen. "You still need work on your writing style," Kina explained (he was always meticulous and mercilessly critical when it came to writing), "but it will do nicely. I will have it sent ahead to Bathill, so it may be presented before Parliament. You'll have to be there next week to impart it formally before the throne and both houses."

Kina didn't say any more after that, he made his way to the closet for his coat and then left.

Ed looked bewildered as he watched his mentor leave.

"What's the matter?" Alice asked.

Ed did not answer. His look of bewilderment quickly changed into a smirk, and then into a grin.

"Ha!" Ed cried, as he slapped his hands together in a loud clap. "We're off to Bathill!"

Chapter V
Bathill, Parliament, and the Temptation of Bug-a-Boo

Not long after Kina had left the house, Ed set straight to work preparing for Bathill. That afternoon, he and the others traveled to the booking office at the railway station in the Older District to reserve tickets for the train and stopped off at Cheswick's to collect some formal wear for their trip. Little Dill insisted on going, he had even gone so far as to show up at Ed's house the night before they were to leave with a small chest packed with clothes. Ed nearly said yes, but Kina intervened, stating he had an important mission for the small toy.

That morning, Ed, Zach, Alice and Travis stood at the platform waiting for the train with George and Emma, who had come along to see the trio off. Emma had given each person a small package of sandwiches for the journey.

"You'll be in for quite a trip," George commented. "Bathill is the cultural centre of the Deltic Empire. I've only been fortunate to go a few times. The last time I went was during the St. Bryan's Day Riots in '77."

"What was that?" Alice asked.

"A mighty mess if there ever was one." George prattled on. "A few students held a protest over some scandals the Conservatives were embroiled in. Rather then let the students practice their rights, the government had other plans and sent the riot guard on them. What followed was two days of rioting that nearly destroyed the city. All trains heading to Bathill were either stopped or ordered to return to their previous station."

After a few minutes, a perky little tank engine shunted the coaches in front of the platform, each one painted purple and cream with the words *Imperial Rail* layered upon their sides. When the tank left, a large and majestic steam locomotive with the name *Behemoth* stamped on her tender backed down onto the train.

"This is the point where things go from familiar to strange," commented Ed, as a faun dressed as a guard walked out of one of the carriages. "Newtown is about as close to our world as it gets here, but in Bathill you'll think you've entered a modern-day Middle Earth."

Soon, more people began to appear on the platform and fill the coaches. Ed, Alice, Zach and Travis were led to their booked compartment in the rear coach. After what felt like hours, the guard blew their whistle and the train pulled out of the station, white smoke escaping from its sides and black and grey pouring from its funnel enveloped the engine and everything surrounding. The quartet looked out of the window and watched George and Emma wave them off through the steamy haze as *Behemoth* rumbled out of the station and into the Deltic countryside.

The engine moved across the countryside at high speed. Stone houses and sleepy barns stood solemnly like bulwark sentinels against the brown and yellow hills. Horses galloped beside them doing their best to keep up, but soon lost the race as the engine crossed the Tashford[13] River and entered the township of New Vin. There, *Behemoth* was uncoupled from her burden and a fresh engine, named *Eagle*, was coupled to the train.

"*Eagle* never enters Newtown," Ed explained, in a matter-of-fact way. "She's owned by the Imperial Railway while *Behemoth* is owned by the Newtown, Electon and Prong Railway. To save people from having to jump from one train to another, *Behemoth* provides the service of bringing the train to New Vin, which is on the border of Imperial Rails' mainline."

No one seemed to be listening, however. They were mesmerized by the elegance, beauty and strange-yet-familiar-ness of the scenery. This sense of wonder was seen especially in Bridgington,[14] a large city built upon a series of bridges over swampland. The

---

[13] Pronounced T/ash/ford

[14] Pronounced Bridge/ing/ton

train journeyed along the streets and mingled with the crowds of people, traveling at a slow speed. Passengers wishing to get off the train would merely open the doors of their coach and step out. Ed explained that a station was never established in Bridgington, so it seemed logical to allow people to walk in and out of the train as the engine moved at a slow pace.

After Bridgington, the engine made its way at full speed for Bathill, the capital of the Deltic Empire. The route was steep as the *Eagle* made her way up a series of hills. The final and steepest part of the route proved to be the most challenging with black smoke erupting from her funnel as she drew closer to the goal and loud chuffing that could be heard for miles.

"Long ago in the times before the empire," Ed explained poetically, "the Deltic tribes settled at a reservoir where the Tashford and Dunbar rivers met. These tribes named the highest point after their leader Bathtic, and thus Bathtic's Hill, or *Bathill*, was born."

As Ed finished, the engine completed her climb and let out a shrill cry from her whistle in triumph. From their coach on the crest of the hill, everyone looked out to see a massive lake where a majestic city rested at its shores. Among the menagerie of various buildings was a wide boulevard that ran from the harbour to a luxurious palace at the top of a hill. Dotting the road were gigantic lamps that ran along the middle and stopping before the palace.

"That's Beacon's Run," Ed explained. "It's the oldest district in the city. In the past, the lamps served as warning markers of a threat coming."

The engine entered St. Oliver's Station, where the elegant stone pillars and stained-glass windows greeted the travelers as they departed from the coaches. At the main doors of the station, Ed flagged down a taxi, and directed the driver to take them to the Empress Hotel.

As the taxi puttered along the streets to its destination, Alice, Zach, and Travis observed the world around them. The various buildings stood like a great wall of stone and glass along the sides of the road while creatures of various types walked the streets dressed in robes, cloaks, starched collars, loose shirts, tight shirts, frocks, clogs, boots, and various other garbs one would wear. At the same time, the smells of spice merchants, brewers, bakers, smokers, and other odious sources wafted into the cab. To the young trio, Bathill could have been any other old city if it hadn't been for the sights of trolls, goblins, elves, ogres, dryads, and other otherworldly beings that walked among the streets.

At last, the taxi came to a halt in front of a mammoth structure of white stone decorated in a variety of coloured trim while tall ornate pillars stood like tree trunks to support the mighty canopy that branched out from the main building. On either side of the main doors were the flag of the Gallan-Gallet—a gold four-point star over a background of green and red with a thick bar of purple-blue on either side—and the flag of the Deltic empire— the same gold star over green and red with a bar of purple-blue beneath with bars of purple, orange and beige next to it.

"Here we are!" Ed announced as everyone pulled themselves out from inside the taxi.

A nearby porter spotted the quartet exiting the car and ran to assist in collecting their baggage. Once the trunks and cases were loaded onto a trolly, Ed, Zach, Travis, and Alice all made their way into the hotel.

The interior of the Empress was the definition of elegance. Large white walls were lined with gold trim, tall pillars of marble supported the high ceilings, and great marble stairs rose upwards from the main lobby to the many floors above. In the centre was a large statue of a woman who looked like a much ruder version of Queen Victoria with a scowling face, holding a sceptre in her right hand. The brass label on the base of the statue read:

QUEEN FLORANCE
1817-1897
EMPRESS OF THE DELITC EMPIRE
1834-1897

Portraits of prominent guests lined the walls with little placards explaining who they were, while the floors were lined wall-to-wall with lush carpeting.

The guests were sights in themselves. Elves, dwarves, nymphs and even animals walked about in fine clothes.

Zach, Alice and Travis were all amazed to see a troll and goblin in a hot debate over the price of imported goods while an elf and a dwarf played a heated game of checkers in a corner.

After checking in and finding their suite—a huge space with several private rooms and a large bathroom—everyone attended to their own devices. While Alice took the bathroom hostage to enjoy a much sought-after bath, Ed, Travis and Zach relaxed in the lounge room. The three men sat drinking a concoction called Ja'goo[15], a pinkish liquid that tasted similar to black tea with strong flavours of vanilla and mint. "A delicacy from the Dominion of Simon'ah." Ed had explained.

"Now what?" Zach asked.

"We relax," Ed answered. "Tomorrow will be a long one. We have to make our rounds about Parliament and meet with Guthrie Bloom."

"Guthrie Bloom?" piped Travis.

"He's an odd fellow, so I've heard but I've never met him." Ed explained, as he drew a complimentary cigar from an ornate box nearby. "He's the MP for the Newtown, Electon, and New Vin riding. Without him, we wouldn't have the support of the Working-Class Party or the Unionists. We'll have to meet with him to get a lay of the field before the meeting. Her Majesty, Queen Clair II will be attending this meeting with both halls."

---

[15] Pronounced J/ah/gō

"Yer gonna have to give a crash course on all this," Zach insisted.

"It's all quite simple," Ed explained. "The Deltic Empire's government is a constitutional monarchy – like Canada or Great Britain – made up of several political parties: the Methodist Party, Working Class Party, Liberal Party, Unionist and Conservative. These parties exist in both halls of Parliament."

"And what are those?"

"What are what?"

"The *halls*."

"Oh! Yes, of course. The Parliament of the Deltic Empire is divided into two parts or "halls," the hall of elected officials, the "Hall of Commons," and the hall of permanent members, the "Hall of Honours." Think of it like Britain, with its House of Commons and House of Lords. The only difference here is that both have a cabinet that can propose policies and vote on bills."

They did very little for the rest of the night. There was a short game of cards and then they went to bed, knowing that the next day would be busy.

The following morning, everyone woke early. As they were going to Parliament, they all had to dress in fine attire—the men in suits and Alice in a dress. Once they were ready, Ed sent a request to the front desk for a taxi and the group crowded in for Parliament.

The long drive was an entertaining one. People and animals walked up and down the sidewalks in various forms of fashion, and the buildings displayed architecture from various time periods. The taxi halted before an elaborately-decorated iron gate with the words "Deltus Imperium" affixed to it in the rune-like letters that seemed to mark everything on the island. Ed, Zach, Alice and Travis left the taxi and followed the cobblestone path into a structure made up of a roof with a series of columns supporting it its weight.

"This is Issacon's hall," explained Ed. "We just have to follow this to the very end, and we will be at the offices."

The group followed this route to the centre where it branched out left and right, forming a large square with stone buildings on each side. They weren't the only ones there, though. People, animals, elves, dwarves and other mystic figures walked about, some standing and talking to each other, some running to one of the three buildings. In the middle of the courtyard was a massive stone figure holding a stone scroll; a plaque underneath read:

WILIAM ISSACON (1857-1936)
SAVOUR OF THE EMPIRE

"Who's that?" asked Travis, pointing to the statue.

"That's Sir William Issacon, the first king that was not from the royal lineage of the Gore family after the

Deltics decided they didn't want hereditary rulers. They did return to the old way of doing things, however. In fact, Her Majesty, Clair II, is the first Gore family member to ascend to the throne after the reform."

Ed stopped to ask a lion the direction to Guthrie Bloom's office, and they made their way into one of the buildings. All the buildings were similar, the halls were decorated with multiple paintings—mostly of former monarchs, late elder statesmen, and scenes from the empire's history. Each door was of raw umber with the occupant's name printed in gold on a black card, affixed with a nail.

The group walked through the halls until they came across a sign that read:

Sir Guthrie L. Bloom
QC, MP, PC, KDE
Working Class Party
Party Leader
Chief Whip of Her Majesty's Opposition

Ed knocked on the door until there was a gruff call of, "Enter."

The room was nicely furnished. At one end was a writing desk with a large bookshelf behind it. On the other end was a set of comfortable chairs with a coffee table in the middle. Behind the desk sat a man who looked to be in his forties—but must have been much older—in a suit with a pair of glasses sitting at the end of his nose. This man was Guthrie Bloom.

Bloom glared up from behind his glasses. "Good to see you, Mr. Worsley," the politician said, as he stood up to shake hands.

After the introductions were made, the group sat around the coffee table and Bloom got right to business.

"A well-written report," Bloom said. "You have the support of the Working-Class Party and the Unionists. The Conservatives and Liberalists haven't said anything yet and the Methodists are outright against the report."

"I was never expecting the Methodists to support us," Ed replied.

"They've always been tough nuts to crack." Bloom said, reflectively. "Anywa', have you a minister and lord yet? You know the Methodists and Conservatives will want you to stick to the rules of the *Beckett Act*."

"The wha'?" Zach said, confusedly.

"Only the most important act in the name of Deltichood," Bloom replied, proudly. "The *Beckett Act* is a law outlining the regulations for report presentations in the Deltic Parliament. In section 91 Subsection C, 'all presenters must have the support of one Member of Parliament and one Lord or Honourable Member. If the presenter is from outside of the Deltic Empire, they must have the political equivalents from their home country's legislative and executive branches.'"

Zach, Travis and Alice looked puzzled.

"Oh, yes," Ed replied. He then pointed with his thumb toward the trio.

"Them?"

"Oh, yes," explained Ed. "Tell me, Guthrie, have you ever heard of Sealand?"

"Sealand?"

"It's a small principality from my world."

Guthrie tried to play along. The old politician's world was very aware of other realms, and he knew that Ed was not from this one. With a brief pause to moisten his lips and figure out how to word his next sentence, the old politician asked: "Which one is which?"

"Travis is an M.P. for one of their constituencies and Zach, well, he happens to be a lord."

Travis and Zach looked flabbergasted.

"Is it a respected state?" Bloom asked, wanting more information.

"One of the most." Ed went on. "It's considered a cultural and national example to all others."

"I would like to further this discussion," went on Bloom, as he checked his wristwatch, "but I have a cabinet meeting to attend to iron out a few things for tomorrow. I'll make sure to have my clerk telephone you when we know the exact time and any other particulars."

As the quartet left the office, Bloom turned to Travis and Zach. "It was an honour to meet the two of you. Sir," Bloom shook Travis' hand and then tuned to Zach and gave a curt bow, "and your lordship."

"Lord?" grumbled Zach. It was all he could say the rest of the day. Travis was, on the other hand, used to being strung up in Ed's schemes and fraud seemed like a new field of expertise.

"It'll work, I think." Ed said trying to sound reassuring. They had returned to the hotel after a day of meetings with prominent members of government and members of the order.

"I think he's worried about being caught," commented Alice apathetically from behind a newspaper.

"You won't," Ed promised. "This is only a formality; the government doesn't have the legal right to give you three background checks. I could say you were the King of Bristolburg, or Chester-Stan-Stan, for all I wanted."

Zach was still unsure. As tempting as it would be to pretend to be a lord, the repercussions could be dire. "What am I required to do?" he asked, still clinging onto a fair-sized sliver of caution.

"Nothing, I'll be doing all the talking. You two only give me legitimacy in the house. There is one thing the Connies and the Methos like, and that is legitimacy."

Before Zach could say more, there came a knock at the door. Ed went to answer; it was a pixy in a maroon uniform and a small cap on its head.

"Is a Mr. Wesley Axelthorp in?" the pixy asked.

"Yes." Ed replied, remembering the pseudonym that Kina had put the group under.

"There's a visitor in the main lobby requesting to speak with you. Something about government business."

"Ah"—Ed replied and looked back to his friends—"I'll be right back."

When the three were left alone, a certain voice called out: "He can be a right ass sometimes, you know."

Everyone looked up. It was Bug-a-Boo. The old wizard stepped out of the fireplace with a red carpetbag.

"I know I was defending him last time, but I absolutely hate it when he gets all cocky."

"What are you doing here?" cried Alice.

"Getting you lot out of here before it is too late," the wizard replied. "Ed has no right getting you three entangled within otherworldly politics."

"But Ed's already counting on us," protested Alice.

"He'll have to deal with it on his own," Bug-a-Boo snapped. "It isn't right for you three to be brought into this."

"I'm not going," shot back Zach.

"Neither am I," put in Travis.

"And why ever not?" asked Bug-a-Boo, curiously. "You certainly didn't seem all that certain before, Zacchaeus."

"We've made a commitment," Zach argued. "We can't just leave Ed like this."

"You three have no right to be pulled into this situation," Bug-a-Boo argued. "It would be far better to get you three out before it's too late."

"Are you deaf?" Zach fired back, growing annoyed. "We said we aren't leaving. Now, go take your rat bag and parlour tricks back to wherever it is you come from."

Bug-a-Boo did not like hearing this. The long pipe between the wizard's teeth began to spew red and black smoke, and in a deep, hard-to-contain voice, he replied: "Two things, boy" – glaring at Zach as he said this. "First, you seemed pretty unhappy about coming here at the start, I was just trying to help you out. Second, never—and I mean never—cross a wizard. We have a tendency of being…unforgiving."

Before anyone could say anything, the smoke from Bug-a-Boo's pipe began to consume him as it had before and then he was gone. As Bug-a-Boo faded out, Ed came into the room.

"I was just speaking to a dignitary from Parliament," Ed explained. "We are to speak at the afternoon session tomorrow." After saying what he needed to say, Ed left to his room.

The three looked at each other. They couldn't put their finger on why, but Ed seemed a little upset as he left.

Chapter VI
Parliament

The following morning, everyone had to wake up early to prepare for their trip to parliament. Alice was dressed in a light and flowy Aegean blue tea dress that was cut at the base of her neck, with a simple navel length pearl necklace that bounced about as she moved. To complete the ensemble, a wide brimmed hat made of straw and ornated with a silver ribbon sat neatly atop her brown hair. Ed, Travis and Zach had to dress in morning suits with stiff starched collars and fronts. Ed was able to slip quite easily into the suit, while Zach and Travis' shirtfronts kept uncoupling from the back-collar stud, not to mention the strangulation they felt by the heavily-starched collar. Other parts of their attire proved to have problems of their own as well.

Zach's face went red with frustration as he struggled to button the pants. "These fit when we were in Newtown!" Zach fumed.

"It's okay," Alice joked, "we all put on a few pounds now and again."

"I haven't gained anything," Zach insisted. "These pants don't even reach my ankles. Their shorts if anything."

Travis walked out of his room. The bottoms seemed to flop about on the floor and hang from the suspenders. "I believe there was a mix-up," said Travis politely.

Once everyone was finally ready, they went down to the entrance of the hotel to take a private car to a restaurant for breakfast. It was empty, for the most part, except for a few people seated at one table. In a corner was a bar that was closed until the later part of the day, where a waiter was wiping the brass on the bar with polish. When he saw the group, he quickly brought them to a table.

While they were conversing and waiting for their orders to arrive, Ed was scanning through his copy of the report and scribbling, scratching and re-editing it in a frantic action. Every time he would reach the last page, he would flip back to the beginning and revise the report again.

No one knew what to say, Ed had been so over-confident during their time in Newtown, but now he seemed tremendously nervous here in Bathill. His hands shook all the way through breakfast.

After they'd finished eating, they climbed into their private car and were taken to the main entrance of Parliament. The cab rolled along a cobblestone road, traveling through another set of gates to enter a courtyard where, in the centre, some maintenance workers were cleaning an ancient cannon on a stone platform. When the car finally reached the end of the courtyard, it stopped before a long series of steps leading up to the main doors.

As Ed, Travis, Zach and Alice walked up the stairs, they passed many of the same creatures from the day before. Many were dressed in black gowns, silk jabots around their collars and coloured sashes across their waistcoats to indicate their party status. Guthrie Bloom, who had a friend with him to escort Alice to the viewing gallery, quickly found them. When Alice had left, Bloom gave the three men all the information he had on where the parties stood in their support of the report.

"The Working Class and Liberals are in favour; they'll both be voting as a block. The Methodist, they're intending to vote against it as a block. I still have no clue about the Conservatives and Unionists, though, they seem to be keeping things quite secretive this time and keep changing their minds."

"I thought you had this all figured out the day before?" Zach inquired.

"A lot happens in a night in the world of politics." Bloom replied defensively. "It also doesn't help that the Earl of Neely has threatened to lead a veto should we move to a vote. Lord Hucklestone is working diligently to quell that chance of rebellion."

"Sounds like our work might not be nearly as easy as I thought," Ed said, sounding somewhat concerned.

The chamber that both houses were to meet in was vast and heavily laid with woodcarvings along the panels in front of the seats for the Deltic politicians while marble pillars stretched up to the ceiling. On the far end of the chamber was an ancient and elegant chair made of sturdy wood with gold lining along the edges in a decretive pattern. Ed, Zach and Travis were directed to sit in a set of chairs on one side of the hall. The three men looked uncomfortable with the strong lights that were cascading hot radiance upon them.

Alice waited up in the viewing gallery, watching the events unfold. Ed had given her a general outline of the occasion while Bloom's friend told her each person that was entering.

Two pages approached the heavy oak doors to the chamber—each grabbing a long red rope attached to either door—to allow the large procession to enter at the sound of two trumpet toots. First entered the Lord Beadle, Sir Randal Parkwith, Master of the Holly Rod, a rotund fellow who seemed overheated by his heavy gown and cocked hat and winded as he lugged his gold staff up the center isle. Alice nearly started laughing as the fat fellow made her think of Charles Dicken's Mr. Bumble.

Ed leaned over to Zach. "Watch," he whispered, "The old man is going to sneak a gin from his flask in a second."

Sure enough, the Lord Beadle paused to mop his face with a handkerchief and making a half-hearted salute, Zach noticed the thin sliver of metal that could have been part of a flask. Upon being refreshed, the Lord Beadle returned his flask in quick succession to the inside pocket of his coat and continued his march.

Following the Lord Beadle was the Lord Chancellor, Lord Eton Devram, a tall and lean man dressed in a long-powdered wig and gold trimmed robes.

"The Lord Chancellor is the most powerful post under the crown," Ed continued to explain. "They lead the Privy Council and oversee all the administration of the civil service."

His lordship was not impressed by the drunken attitude of the Lord Beadle. He became red-faced and cross when he nearly bumped into the Lord Beadle and held a look on his face that suggested that he wanted to kick his predecessor. After the Lord Chancellor came two stewards, each carrying a massive mace, one gold and the other silver. Following the two stewards were the Speakers in black gowns and lace jabots like their fellow colleagues, only with gold trim lining the edges of their gowns like the Lord Chancellor and each wore a Welsh wig atop their heads. Afterward came the Prime Minister and Governor General of the Deltic Empire, each wearing fur gowns over their suits.

"The Right Honourable Samuel Holland," the Lord Chancellor announced, "Prime Minister of the United Crown Island of the Gallan-Gallet and the Chancellor of the Deltic Empire! The High Honourable Lord Daniel Jackson, Earl of St. Wells-by-Northford, Governor General of the Crown Island of the Gallan-Gallet and Lord Protector to all Realms of the Deltic Empire!"

Once they had taken their seats, trumpets sounded, and the Lord Beadle rose, staggering slightly from the influence of whatever substance was in his flask.

"Minsh'er-sh and Lord-sh," the red-faced Lord Beadle slurred loudly. "Heel!"

"It's *hear* you drunk oaf." the Lord Chancellor whispered, becoming more embarrassed.

"Hear!" the Lord Beadle went on. "Her maje-shty approaches!"

The trumpets blasted another cry of fan fair and Her Majesty Queen Clair II, Queen of the United Crown Island of the Gallan-Gallet, Protectorate of the Dominion of Simon'ah, and Empress of the Deltic Empire, entered the chamber, dressed strictly in what was deemed acceptable for Parliament. Upon her shoulders was the custom red fur gown and upon her head the golden crown, which shimmered in the pale lights that shone from above. As the Queen walked into the chamber, all the members of the Halls of Commons and Honours stood to attention and sang the Imperial

Anthem, which was played on an organ from another chamber.

> One mighty kingdom, safe to all!
> Bulwark of old, ne'er to fall!
> All hail, the provider of good desire;
> All hail, the Deltic Empire!
>
> Dominion of beauty, of mountains so dear;
> Valleys of innocence, waters so clear.
> Praise, for the land that was oh so required;
> Praise to the realms of the Deltic Empire!
>
> One crown of union of the Queen;
> Sacred diadem of freedom sing!
> Bow to the might of the throne;
> Bow to the protector of our home!

The music died away, and everyone sat in their places. One of the stewards, dressed in a green gown with white trimming, stood and read from a roll of parchment: "On this day of our blessed Queen, we join for the closing of this session of Parliament. We shall be hearing a presentation from the Order of the Four Keepers, followed by a speech from the throne before concluding."

One of the Speakers–a grizzly looking fellow–stood and called out gruffly: "Is their presenter within these halls?"

Ed stood to attention. "I am!" he called back.

"Have you your supporters?"

"I do."

Zach and Travis both stood.

"Your supporters may be seated," the steward ordered. "You may present your report before the Parliament."

The members of the Deltic Parliament watched with attention as Ed spoke. The facts of the matter were quite simple. The people of the city of Apothem had mysteriously vanished from the Finylands. The accounts from those outside and the surviving recorded messages from within the city reported a large purple cloud descending upon Apothem. The description of this cloud met the description of the Manookoo cult's cloud from Zeltic myth. Other reports were claiming that the cloud was on route to the Gallan-Gallet.

"What are you suggesting?" called a politician with the face of a bullfrog.

"I am suggesting," replied Ed, choosing his words carefully, "that our very empire is under threat from forces unknown."

"This is nonsense!" the frog-faced man cried, looking at the speaker. "Honourable Speaker, are we to have our time wasted for some children's bedtime story? Are we to be sent up to our beds after the meeting is convened?"

"Here, here!" billowed a few voices.

"Her Majesty's time"—the frog-faced man continued— "and the Parliament's time are being wasted with falsehoods and rumours made by the Order of the Four Keepers to usurp the our legitimacy as protectors of this empire."

"Honourable Speaker!" called Bloom, from his side of the house. "Might I remind the honorable member that it is this gentleman and his two companions who are giving the presentation and not he himself?"

The council broke out into intense argument. Half of the house was calling for immediate action while the other claimed Ed's comments were merely fear-mongering from the Order of the Four Keepers. The Earl of Neely stood to his feet and began making a long-winded speech about his views on the matter while Lord Hucklestone, another lord and several members of parliament attempted to pull him back to his seat. A red-faced bishop began bullying a member of parliament over what was they thought the truth of the matter was and demanded that the member agree with them.

At last, Her Majesty arose. The Lord Chancellor noted this and swatted the Lord Beadle, who had dozed off during the presentation.

"Silence!" the Lord Beadle bellowed and slammed the bottom of his staff on the marble floor, erupting a load clatter what overpowered the arguing aristocrats and politicians. The Lord Chancellor went red with embarrassment and held his ears.

The chamber became quiet.

"It appears," the Queen began, sounding demure and blunt, "we are at a standstill. Would you not agree, Prime Minister?"

"It appears so, Your Majesty."

"And our Governor General?"

"I quite agree, Your Majesty."

The Queen turned her attention to Ed, Zach and Travis. "Young man, how long do you think we will have until this cloud appears here?"

"I would estimate, based upon what happened in Apothem, at the earliest a week or so at the least, Your Majesty." Ed replied promptly. "There is no sure sign of how long it will take to arrive, only that we must be ready."

"Is there anything within this cloud that would pose a specific threat to anyone?" the Queen asked.

"Yes. While the initial myth about Spyrus and the Manookoo only allude to this, other translations and sources suggest that the very cult members were mutated into accursed creatures who are to hunt upon any souls they wish to feed upon."

Her majesty shuddered for a moment but recovered. "Then parliament will not close," proclaimed the Queen. "I order both houses to meet in session tomorrow and discuss the matter. If what this young man says is true, I would advise clear, sober thought on the matter."

The parliamentarians erupted in a rumble of disagreement.

"Clear, sober thought, gentlemen!" the Queen erupted, ushering the parliament back into silence. The queen then turned her attention to Ed, Zach and Travis. "Thank you, gentlemen, for this report. I can only promise that my government will look into this matter."

The Lord Beadle stamped his rod three times and the trio were led out of the chamber by an armed steward.

"That went well," said Zach, to no one in particular, as the large oak doors closed behind them.

"Yes," agreed Ed. "That is why I suggest we skip town while the going is good."

"What?"

"The face of Augustus Maverton projected a seething hatred for us."

"Who?"

"Maverton, the guy with the ugly face who asked what I was suggesting."

Travis and Zach gave a look that suggested they both did and didn't understand what their friend was saying.

"Maverton," continued Ed, with an air of gravity, "is head of the Royal Secret Police. He does not like people suggesting the Empire is under threat, that's his job. I won't be surprised if we are arrested tonight."

"So, we're leaving?" asked Travis.

"Yep," answered Ed as he checked his watch, briefly. "Right now, actually. Bloom has arranged a cab for us, and our things will be at the station, that's who I was meeting with last night in the lobby. We shall be riding the *Evening Star*; it'll have us home by morning. It's a good thing I never submitted our *real* names."

"What do you mean?" inquired Travis.

"I usually go by pseudonyms when in Bathill. You know, John Marrick, Brian Wilson, Joseph Bennett... stupid names to cover up our appearances."

As the three departed the doors, Travis realized something important. "What about Alice?"

"Oh, she'll be fine," assured Ed. "Her escort is a member of the Order. Bloom has given him strict instructions to take her to the station as soon as we left the chamber."

"Damn, you thought of everything didn't you," Zach said, impressed.

"Only when the Secret Police may be on our tails," Ed rebuked. "Now, come on!"

They made a speedy walk from the halls of parliament to the main gate where sure enough a cab was awaiting their arrival. As soon as everyone could get in, the cab made a charge out of the court yard and rumbled out of the large gates. All the while, Zach and Travis set to work loosening their ties and unclasping their collars for comfort!

The cab screeched to a halt in front of St. Oliver's Station and the trio bolted to inside to meet with Alice and Bloom's friend.

"Mr. Sawyer!" Ed called as he Zach and Travis met the pair.

Mr. Sawyer looked much younger than the quartet, twenty years old at the most. He wore a top coat that was buttoned up to the very top and a cap plopped on the top of his head. He made no time noticing Ed and company. "Good to see you Mr. Worsley," he greeted. "How was the meeting?"

"Long and cumbersome." Ed replied as he and everyone else made their way up to the platform. "I think there's some hope and I think the Deltic parliament will see sense… I hope."

"Shall I send that in my wireless to the Director?"

"You can send that to Kina and a few other things I would tell but I've a train to catch."

Before Mr. Sawyer could say more, Ed, Alice, Zach, and Travis dashed through the gates to the platform and hoped into the first train before them.

The four friends sat in their compartment of the train. The enchanted coaches served them their tea and supper as the engine made its long, weighty voyage to Newtown by going north to the moorlands and stopping in a city called St. Wells before another train took over to travel along the Tashford River. It was, as Ed put it, the long way home but it was the best way to get there without anyone expecting them.

Over supper, Ed shared the story of the Canker, the fallen star who was captured by Kon-luk, the warrior of the Deltics. Kon-Luk wanted to fight the ghost of the warrior Lomassmay, in order to gain the strength of a thousand men and hoped that in capturing a star he would be able to wish the ghost before him. Canker tricked Kon-luk into freeing him by telling him the ghost of Lomassmay would only appear to those who proved themselves honourable. In order to prove he was an honorable warrior, Kon-luk was told by Canker to free him, and the ghost of Lomassmay would appear. In doing so, Kon-Luk never got his wish, nor did he ever see the ghost of Lomassmay.

It was dark now and the stars were beginning to come out. Ed sat staring out at the black abyss as everyone else slept.

Chapter VII
Little Dill's Army

~*~

The group returned to Newtown just after midnight. Ed made sure the house was locked up tightly when they were home. A news article in the *Imperial Star*—a Deltic newspaper—outlining an attempted arrest at the Empress Hotel in Bathill the night they had left the city proved Ed's prediction of possible capture. That morning, Ed and Travis sat in the living room. As everyone else was asleep, the two young men had decided to discuss what they should do next.

"There isn't much we *can* do," Ed explained. "Parliament will debate the matter and decide what course will be taken. I just hope Bloom was able to work his influence."

"I guess we can chill 'til then," concluded Travis. "There's no use worrying about something we don't know anything about."

"True. I guess we could go to the river, it's quite nice this time of year," Ed suggested, as he looked up at the clock.

Ed and Travis made their way to the kitchen for breakfast. As soon as Ed put the kettle on the stove, Ryan came in from work.

"Morning, gents," he announced and collapsed into one of the chairs in the kitchen, making quite a bit of unwelcomed racket when he did so.

"Shh!" snapped Ed. "Zach and Alice are still sleepin'."

Ryan said nothing else and picked up the paper, noisily rustling it as he flipped through the pages.

Travis jumped when he spotted Little Dill at the kitchen window. He almost did not recognize the small toy this time, as Little Dill was dressed in an orange cardigan and a blue collarless shirt instead of his familiar purple coat and yellow vest. The toy waved excitingly as Travis opened the window. Little Dill then proceeded to jump from the counter to the kitchen table and take a seat on top of a saltshaker.

"Mr. Kina's beens keeping me busy," Little Dill explained, in his usual way.

"With what?" asked Travis.

"I can't says. It's top secrets," answered Little Dill before taking a surprisingly large bite out of a slice of toast.

"I can't imagine what Kina would have you do," commented Ryan, from behind the paper. "You're only useful for typing, and even then, you wear yourself out dancing on the keys."

Little Dill's face grew red at this. "You takes that backs!" he snapped.

"Why would I take back the truth? I mean, you're too small for Kina to have any *real* use for you, he only has you in the Order because you have better grammar and spelling than the other typists."

Little Dill began throwing sugar cubes at Ryan with as much force as he could muster. Each cube just bounced off and landed on either Ryan's lap or the table. The small doll was so busy with his fit of fury that he did not notice Ed grab him by the back of his orange coat.

"Why do you have to provoke him like that?" Ed asked Ryan, as he placed Little Dill on the counter.

"Can't help it," said Ryan, with a cheeky grin. "It's just fun getting him going."

The hectic fight between Little Dill and Ryan woke Zach and Alice, who joined the others downstairs. Over their breakfast, the quartet made plans to travel to the river for some sightseeing. When they finished, they made their way down the street to a small dirt road that branched out toward a nearby forest.

The Tashford Forest, in all its glory, is located just outside of Newtown near the Tashford River. Though it was often full of holidaymakers, in the autumn haze it was quiet and peaceful. The river still hadn't frozen over and there were two or three people on the other side of the river fishing, trying to get a few more catches before the ice began to build up. As the group of four wandered through the area, each keeping to their own devices, they noticed the mud and dead leaves mixing with the light sprinkling of snow that had fallen the night before.

Ed took a seat on a bench, observed the quiet scenery, and slowly drifted into meditation. He watched Travis and Zach walking along the bank and throwing stones into the river, and Alice walking among the trees. As they enjoyed themselves, some children came running up to Ed.

"'Cuse me mis'er," said one, "but our ball's fallen into the wa'er and's stuck on a branch. Could you get it for us?"

Ed called Travis, Zach and Alice to join him. The ball in question was caught on a tree branch and was bobbing about in the water. A plan was quickly made; Travis, while holding on to Zach and Ed, would reach over to the ball and collect it. It seemed like a simple plan, but if any lesson can be taken from this situation, it's that the simplest things can be the biggest headaches.

Travis leaned out for the ball, which turned out to be further out than first thought. Zach and Ed moved forward a bit to help Travis. The mud beneath their feet began to make them slide, and the next thing they knew, the three men tumbled into the river.

"I got it!" cried Travis, as Zach and Ed sat picking dead leaves from their hair.

"I don't know what you three were thinking," called George, from inside the kitchen. "Going into the Tashford River at this time of the year...you're lucky Pumpkin Stone and I was heading down there."

They were at the McTrotter home. George and Pumpkin Stone had been out for a walk when they came across Ed, Alice, Zach and Travis at the riverbank. At George's insistence, everyone headed to the McTrotter house to warm up. George loaned the men some dry clothes while Emma tended to the wet ones.

Ed, Zach and Travis all sat on a couch by the blazing fire with large, thick blankets wrapped around them for warmth.

George emerged from the kitchen with a tray of mugs and handed one to Ed, Zach and Travis each. The mugs contained a greyish fluid, which the young men drank down and immediately spat out.

"What's in this?" shot Zach, in disgust.

"Just an old family recipe," replied George. "My mother used to make it when we had the sniffles. Tea, honey, mustard, salt and vinegar. You never forgot your jacket and boots when you left the house after having a dose of that."

"It's not too bad if you can move it around your tongue," muttered Ed to the other two. "Kind of has a tolerable aftertaste, if I do say so myself."

"Have you seen Little Dill lately?" George added as he took a seat and filled his pipe with tobacco. "The wee thing was here not too long ago and when he left, some of our cutlery was gone. Even the Hudson's from up the street have been robbed."

"He did say Kina had put him to work," piped in Travis.

"But what job would Kina put Little Dill up to that includes nicking people's silverware?" inquired George.

"If it's anything, those brownies will be in on it," added Ed. "They always like being up to mischief when there's nothing to do."

"I'm not going to go about accusing brownies of robbing houses." George rebuked. "From my experience their fairly good folk, albeit a little too determined to do house work when they come to visit." George paused to light his pipe and added: "If you do find Little Dill, tell him Emma and I just want our silver back."

That night, the group returned to Ed's house. Alice stood outside looking down the sloped grassy plain of the backyard. In the far-left corner sat the tool shed, an old wooden building that was losing some of its slate panels from the roof. What attracted Alice's attention to it were the strange sounds coming from within the shed.

The noise sounded like someone was rummaging through the shed. Alice slowly made her way to the shack, making sure not to create any noises as she moved. The closer Alice got to the shed, the clearer the sounds became.

"This won't do," called one voice from inside the shed.

"We could use this shovel," went another.

"Nah," said the third. "Remember the last shovel were found? I'm having a repeat of last time."

Alice looked in. She saw three small figures, about the same size as Little Dill, searching through Ed's tool shed. They were dressed in clothes made from bits of rag and other random materials with pointed hats on the tops of their heads. The two figures turned and looked at Alice.

"Run!" called the first and jumped with the second through a convenient nearby hole. The third was not as lucky. It darted for the window at the back of the room, but only crashed into the glass. The sprite, in a state of confusion, darted for the door but was caught by Alice.

"Curse those coattails!" it fumed.

Alice wasted no time bringing the little figure to Ed and the others.

"I should have figured it would be a brownie," said Ed, crossly.

"Master Dill won't like this," snapped the sprite, and kicked over a peppershaker.

"What is it?" asked Zach as he entered the kitchen.

"A brownie." explained Ed. "They're little sprites, usually smaller than gnomes."

"I've got important business to do," the brownie cried.

"I can see that," shot Ed. "Breaking into my shed pitching my gardening tools. I have a good mind to call the police for this."

"Please don't!" cried the brownie again. "Master Dill would not like that. We have to prepare for the invasion!"

"Invasion?"

"Aye, the invasion. Master Kina has given Master Dill instructions to prepare for the invasion of the Milkadoo."

"You mean the *Manookoo*."

"Yeah, that's it."

Ed looked to Alice, Travis and Zach for a brief second and then turned to the brownie. "What is your name, sprite?" he inquired.

"Hob," was the brownie's reply.

"Well, yon sprite Hob," said Ed, being cautious not to offend the brownie. "We would be honoured if you would show us to Lit—I mean, Master Dill."

"I could. But you will have to swear to me that you'll not tell anyone about this."

The way Hob made the quartet swear was strange. First, Hob made them stand on their left foot with their tongues sticking out to swear to the Imp King, then they had to do the same thing on their right foot and swear to the Goblin King. Once this was over, Hob led Ed, Zach, Travis and Alice out to the Tashford Forest.

It was dark when they entered the Tashford. The great, mighty trees looked like long figures with branches like extended fingers, waiting to reach out and snatch them without warning. They were led off the main path into a thicker section of trees. Here, the group began to feel trapped, as the trees became less uniform and began to jeer out in all directions. Alice nearly tripped over a fallen tree as they trekked further in. In the distance, they could hear metal being struck and the smell of burning wood and boiling metal.

The group was greeted with an industrious scene. Great ovens were being fed with coal, wood and any other flammable fuel available, while brownies took turns jumping on handmade billows to keep the fires burning, and others dumped carts loaded with cutlery and garden tools into large caldrons for smelting. The melted metal was then transferred on makeshift cranes to stands, where they were molded and forged into swords, shields, arrowheads and other weaponry.

Overseeing all this work was a small figure standing on a tree branch and dressed in a military uniform. Hob jumped up to the figure and whispered something to it, and then leaped back down to join the others. The figure grabbed what looked like a vine or rope and swung down to where the four stood.

"So, this is what you've been up to, Little Dill," said Ed.

"Hellos," the little toy greeted.

"Looks like you are raising an army," added Travis, stating the obvious.

"Yes, I ams," Little Dill replied, proudly.

"Who put you up to this?" asked Alice.

"Mr. Kina. He tolds me to goes and tells anyone who woulds listen. I wents all over the town withs a sign and no one's listened, except the brownies."

"We could tell," added Ed. "They've been using their ability to enter people's houses to nick cutlery and other metal objects to forge your weapons."

Little Dill looked startled. "You didn't tells me this metals was stolen," the little toy snapped, to a brownie pushing a wheelbarrow.

"You didn't ask," was the brownie's gruff reply, setting off again.

"I didn'ts mean to steals," said Little Dill, still shocked.

"Don't worry," assured Ed. "I'm sure Bug-a-Boo will kindly magic new cutlery and such for those robbed."

"You sures?" Little Dill asked.

"Positive."

After the event in the Tashford Forest, Ed, Travis, Zach and Alice made their way back to the house. Little Dill joined them, as he was too disgusted at the actions of the brownies to continue overseeing their work. Once home, the five sat in the sitting room, sipping some tea while Little Dill told them of his many adventures. As the night grew late, Ed, Alice and Travis left for bed, leaving Zach and Little Dill alone.

"Aren't you scared of going to war?" asked Zach.

"Nope," Little Dill answered, confidently.

Zach was surprised. "How come?"

"I've seen peoples die alls the time. I used to be owned by Bennie-man Frankie-lan's daughter, Sarah."

"Sarah?"

"Yeps. She was my bestest friend, or she used to. When she gots too old for me, I ran away. I traveled all over the colonies; I even saws the revolution. I remember seeing Georgie Washington at Yorktown when Cornie-Wallis surrendered. He was huuuge." Little Dill fell over in his excitement. "Then," he went on, "I wandered some mores and saw the Civil War…"

At this point, Little Dill's voice trailed away. Zach wasn't sure, but he could have sworn there was a tear coming from the doll's eye. "You must have seen a lot of death during that," said Zach.

"Yeah. I can remember walkin' into a small town in the south. There was a little girl theres who found me. Everydays, she would take me to the garden in the back of her homeses. Her names was Margaret. One days, we were playin,' then there cames the sound of gunses and canners. Margaret dropped me as she ran back to the house. I watched as Sherman's Union soldiers burned the whole town to the grounds. Whens I returned to that town later, she was gones. I don't know what happened to her, I've heard that the whole family died in the fire, but I can't believes it…Zachy, I can't stands war. I don'ts like people fighting and killing each other over dumb stuff."

"If you think war is so terrible, why are you raising this army?"

"Someones has to," the little toy replied, will a small amount of passion in his eyes. "I would give up my pacifisms for the chance to save those I love."

Little Dill then looked to the window and stared at the stars; it was the first time anyone had seen Little Dill look sad. Everyone knew the toy was a happy soul—with the habit of getting into trouble now and again—but this subject of war and the remembrance of the horrors of his past made Little Dill show his true side. A side that was masked by a wide grin and flashy coattails, a side saddened by the mere fact that he was almost immortal.

Zach, not knowing what he should do, left the little toy alone.

Chapter VIII
The Call to Arms

~*~

The group sat in the living room. It was long past breakfast and Alice, Zach, Travis and Ed were sitting about watching the television, agreeing it was time for a lazy day. The old tube television was glowing as it showed a rerun of a program called *The Late-Night Variety Show*. A man named Louis Fitzgerald danced about in front of them telling jokes and introducing the next act. Suddenly, the program was interrupted.

The screen changed from the vibrant studio set to an image of the Deltic Parliament building. "We interrupt this program," a bodiless voice announced, "for an urgent bulletin from Bathill, where Prime Minister Samuel Holland is about to make an address the empire."

The image changed to the outside of the palace gates. The Prime Minister stood outside with a sheet of paper in his hand.

"It is with great regret," said the politician, "that I, Prime Minister Samuel Holland, must announce that our great empire has been placed under threat. As of midnight tonight, the United Crown Island of the Gallan-Gallet and her colonies in the Deltic Empire will be at war with an entity that intends to consume all we hold dear..."

Ed look mortified, and before anyone could say anything about it, he had dashed to the kitchen for the telephone. His hands shook as he tried to spin the dial. After several failed attempts, Ed finally put in the correct number.

"Hullo...Kina? Oh, good. I'm guessing you've heard the news. Uh-huh. Lil' Dill will be jumping for the chance to test out his army...I see. When should I go? ...No, that's fine... What about the others? ...I can't just leave 'em...I understand...I'll let you know when he can come."

Ed hung the phone back up. He had not noticed that Alice, Zach and Travis had followed him to the kitchen. Ed looked at his friends, solemnly.

"Kina has given me orders to join Little Dill when he charges for the Manookoo cloud."

"What about us?" asked Zach.

"Your safety can't... it can't be promised. Kina has arranged for Bug-a-Boo to take you all home before it is too late."

"We can't just leave you." piped Alice.

"I don't want to lose any of you," Ed explained. "I would rather send you three home and have you safe than have you all killed."

"But you could die doing this!" cried Travis.

"I guess I'm a fool for not wanting to have people who mean a lot to me get hurt in a war they have nothing to do with."

"Then I guess we are fools, too, for not wanting to leave," said Zach.

Ed looked at his friends. He did not have to say anything, Alice, Zach and Travis knew exactly what it would have been.

"So, you are all going," concluded Bug-a-Boo.

"That's the plan," said Ed.

They were sitting in Ed's study, alone.

"Good. I just want you to know, those three care about you. They're willing to face hellfire and ice for you; people like that are rare in quality, so treat them well. Like a flower, give them light through encouragement and water in the form of loyalty. Alice is your encourager, Travis your confidant, and Zach is your judge. Don't take them for granted."

"I won't," Ed promised.

"Good." Bug-a-Boo was about to draw smoke from his pipe when he paused. "Before I forget, remember what I told you that night at the house: do not cause your lack of awareness be your downfall."

"I won't."

"This is no joke. A premonition was passed to me from an important source. It showed you blind with red rays casting from your sockets. I do not understand its meaning, but you were alone. I won't have you forced to face death alone, I won't able to bring you back here... What I am trying to say is, whether you make it out of this unscathed, I just want you to understand...I will do anything within my power to ensure you and your friends are together."

"You didn't seem too interested in this when we were in Bathill."

Bug-a-boo raised his eyebrows is surprise but quickly recovered. "It is quite true," the wizard admitted, "that I wanted them out of this mess before it got worse. I still feel that they should be sent back, but I can't do such a spell without their consent. If they wish to galivant off and fight off demigods and cursed beasts, then so be it. That said, they are very loyal and I can respect that."

Before Ed could say a word, the wizard was consumed by the smoke of his pipe and was gone.

The group made their way to a small hamlet located next to a wider part of the Tashford River, called Kelton Pass. They were met by Kina who had hired a boat—a rather old tug—for their voyage. Little Dill and his army of brownies were busy loading the boat with supplies, which included non-perishable foodstuffs and weapons, and a radio so they could track the progress of the Deltic Army against the cloud.

"Good luck, you four," said Kina. "Bloom tells me that the warship *Pedigree* is already out at sea and keeping watch for the Manookoo. I advise to reach there as quickly as possible. Bloom will send word through the Ministry of War's channels of your arrival. Wire the Order once you have arrived at the *Pedigree* and leave only when you have received orders from me or by forces beyond our own."

Ed shook hands with Kina. The old professor leaned towards Ed's ear and whispered: "Try not to get yourselves killed."

As Ed, Zach, Alice and Travis journeyed along the Tashford River for the ocean and ultimately the imperial warship *Pedigree*, the government of the Deltic Empire were hard at work making the necessary preparations for the arrival of the Manookoo.

In the office of the Guthrie Bloom, General Blunt (the Minister of War), and Prime Minister Samuel Holland sat around a large desk examining the current status of the situation.

"What is the current state of our military?" the Prime Minister asked.

Blunt stood to attention with an attitude reminiscent of his days as a private in the imperial army. "Our war ship, the *Pedigree*, is making headway toward the Nimbian[16] coast. The *Empress* and the *Leviathan*

---

[16] Pronounced Nim/bee/an

are holding a blockade in the predicted path of the cloud with a few frigates. My associates in the military department have air guns planted in every major city, and trains set up to keep the flow of supplies going. The air force has arranged a series of squadrons to patrol the skies for the cloud. I can say that we've put everything available into this fight. We have several dirigibles acting as central controls while the aeroplanes make a quick job of the Manookoo things."

"This system is quite impressive," Bloom interjected, pragmatically, "but what are we to do if they make landfall."

Blunt leaned forward over the table and pointed to a map of the island, directing them to a series of red lines starting from the Northeastern Coast and making their way inland. "We will be using a series of barrages on land, each acting as a wall while a mass evacuation order will be put in place."

Bloom seemed unconvinced.

Holland turned to Bloom, becoming impatient. "What would you have done when you were prime minister?"

Bloom looked at his successor with a look of grimace. "I'd do the same bloody thing," was his reply. "If we do not act fast in this confrontation, the entire empire is lost."

Across from Bathill, and high above, two men were on a patrol of the skies in a bi-plane. Captain

Smith-Blake and his co-pilot, "Blinky" Rogers, looked about them in normal military fashion, each holding a cup of cocoa to lift their spirits.

They weren't the only ones about. As Blunt had explained, the Imperial Air Force had been dispatched to watch the clouds for the Manookoo. The mighty airship *Avolare* served as a floating base, providing a location for wireless messages to be relayed and as a place for pilots to rest between watches.

Smith-Blake and Blinky had only been sent out a few hours ago on their plane, *Neon Lily*. The pair had only their cocoa and the few snacks they had smuggled aboard from their mothers' care packages.

"Cheese and crackers!" cried Smith-Blake.

"What cap'n?" asked Blinky.

"I thought I squashed the cheese and crackers," replied the captain.

"Oh," replied Blinky. "I hope the jam wasn't damaged, my mother travelled all the way to Little Picking to—"

"OH, HAM!" shouted Smith-Blake. "Look!"

There, in the distance, was a massive cloud. From left to right it seemed endless, its purple hue making it look gigantic. The mass was moving close to the surface of the Periculosus[17] Ocean.

"Take control Blinky!" Smith-Blake ordered. "I've got to radio this into base!"

---

[17] Pronounced Par/ick/los/us

"Righto!"

"Radio to base," called Smith-Blake, to the radio.

On the *Avolare*, a sleepy wireless clerk, who was dozing at his desk, was startled awake by the sound of Smith-Blake's voice.

"This is base," replied the clerk sleepily. "What's your status."

"This is Smith-Blake. We see a tottie[18] straight ahead."

"How fast is the tottie moving?" asked the clerk.

"I estimate twenty minutes from the *Pedigree*."

The clerk scribbled the information on a scrap of paper and waved one of the quartermasters to take it.

The quartermaster studied the information gravely. "Tell 'em to fall back and notify the *Pedigree*," he ordered. "We've no orders to attack just yet."

The clerk nodded as the quartermaster left.

"Base to radio," the clerk rapped, "you've been ordered to fall back. Please notify *Pedigree* and return to your base. Do not in engage. I repeat, do not engage."

"All heard here," Smith-Blake replied. "Good grief! Look at that!"

"Everything alright?" the clerk replied.

No answer.

"Base to radio. Base to radio. Do you hear me?"

Still no answer.

---

[18] Tottie: Deltic military term for a specific target.

What the clerk didn't know was just as the message of the Manookoo's location was sent, a massive creature began to emerge from the cloud. It was some sort of dragon; massive, deformed and blackened. It was this moment, as Smith-Blake sent his final message warning of the creature, that the war for the Deltic Empire had begun.

Chapter IX
The Battle to the Pedigree

~*~

The tugboat charged across the ocean at top speed. Black smoke billowed from its funnel as white and blue slashed the bow. Ed, Alice, Zach, Travis, Little Dill and the army of brownies had heard the message from Smith-Blake of the creature, before his demise along with Blinky and the *Neon Lily*. They had made good time, leaving the Island of the Gallan-Gallet far behind. Little brownies took turns shovelling coal into the ship's boiler, minding the engine and steering the ship—quite a sight to see as they had to stand on one another's shoulders to control the helm.

While all this was happening, Ed and the other four were below deck, each serving their own role in the venture. Little Dill sat in a large swivel chair wearing a pair of oversized headphones, as he dictated the position of the Manookoo and the *Pedigree* to Alice, who marked them out on a map with colour-coded pegs. Ed, Travis and Zach spent most their time wiring Kina in Newtown or Bloom in Bathill; the latest information they had was that the Manookoo had been spotted by the Nimbian Aero-core as they made headway toward the northeastern part of the Gallan-Gallet, and who would intercept the Manookoo soon.

"One, two, three, one, two, three," called a random and unexpected voice. "Confound it! How on Earth do you work these things?"

"It's Buggie-Boo!" cried Little Dill.

Ed grabbed the communication piece. "Ed here," he said. "What can we do for you?"

"I've been studying some accounts of the Manookoo," came the reply. "There is something I've discovered."

"What is it?"

"The rock Spyrus was forged by the Zeltic god Kinmount, god of ice and stone."

"We know that." Ed replied. "One of the books on Zeltic myths George loaned us says that."

"Yes, but there is more." the wizard went on. "I was consulting with a friend of mine when I was shown some lost scribing's on the Spyrus. It is said that in order to warn those who were deemed blessed by Horcus, Spyrus will freeze bodies of water that cross its path."

"In other words?" asked Ed. However, before Bug-a-Boo could say more, the ship shook in a way that suggested that they had run aground. When the quake stopped, Ed, Alice, Zach and Travis found themselves on the floor of the ship. Furniture, papers and books were thrown about; a bookshelf nearly fell on Travis.

When the group had managed to climb up from below decks, they were surprised to find that the boat had landed itself on a vast region of ice, stretching out from them in almost every direction. Many of the brownies were hard at work unloading supplies from the ship onto carts and packs for the next stretch of the journey.

As everyone prepared for the voyage ahead, the sound of some horrific creature could be heard charging across the hazy abyss. Out from the horizon it came, a black snake-like creature, massive and deformed with an arm and a leg emerging from one of its sides, slithering across the plain. Following this monster were several other beings, each deformed in one way or another with the same snake-like oddities.

"Ready yourselves!" called Ed, to the others.

"We'll holds 'em off!" Little Dill cried. "You guys goes ahead to the *Pedigree*."

Ed took one last look at Little Dill. "Good luck, old boy," he said to the toy.

Little Dill saluted and ran to join his army.

Ed, Alice, Zach and Travis watched as the brownies charged forward toward the frightful herd. They wasted no time running along the ice, which was oddly not slippery, to get away from the impending hoard. The group could see that the army of creatures was not nearly as large as they thought. They were now farther from the horde and could continue forward with the use of a compass and a dirty map of the section of sea between the Gallan-Gallet and the Nimbian coast.

It was quiet. The atmosphere about them feeling like at any minute something unpleasant would appear. To the left and right of them was nothing, just clouds of violet and frozen plain. The wind was their only company for this long trip.

No one dared say a word, for fear of their voices becoming their downfall. They had no way of contacting Kina, as the radio from the ship had been damaged when the boat landed and the portable one was in one of the carts with the brownies and had been abandoned when they made their exodus.

Just when they thought they were alone and with not much hope left, something shot down from the sky and flew into Ed, knocking him down. It was a seagull.

"I say," snapped the gull, as it got up and looked around him to see what was about him. "Here I am flying home and what-what, when next thing I know some jiffy dragon and his purple cloud cross my path and separate me from my squadron. Absolutely, crackers, I say."

Zach and Travis helped Ed back up before joining with Alice, who had begun to start a conversation with the white and silver bird.

"Who are you?" asked Alice, ignoring the fact that this gull had crashed into Ed and was making them more exposed to the possibility of another attack.

"Captain Jolly Roger at your service, ma'am," the gull replied, with a bow. "Leader of the Gull Light Air Infantry. My squadron and I were to return to base camp when this cloud appeared out of nowhere. I must say, I've never seen ice on an ocean, though I've never seen ice on any other water, either."

"Have you seen a ship anywhere?" Ed asked, feeling that it would be wise to start moving again soon.

"Oh yes," Jolly Roger replied. "I saw a big grey one not too long ago."

"Would you be able to lead us to it?"

"I could jolly-well try. This cloud makes it hard to know whether I'm east or west. Let me see if I can even fly first."

Jolly Roger moved about to make sure nothing was broken. When all seemed safe, the gull set to the air, making sure that the quartet stayed close by to follow along.

The cloud's vapours made it hard to see where the sun was, which in turn made hard it to determine the time of day; all they knew was that the sun was still up in the sky. In the rush to abandon the boat, some of the supply bags were left behind, leaving the party of four in a desperate situation. With limited supplies and no protection in the event of another attack, everyone was anxious to find the *Pedigree* as soon as possible.

It was getting darker. Jolly Roger was becoming harder to see as they made their way across the ice. But just as they thought their hopes were dashed, the lights from a massive geometric form could be seen. For a brief moment, Jolly Roger disappeared into the black void above as he made his way to the ship, only to glide back to the quartet.

"There she blows, lads!" declared Jolly Roger as he landed before the others. "I told you I would jolly-well get you there!"

By the time Ed, Zach, Travis and Alice reached the warship, night had fallen. The cloud's vapours made the area darker; they were able to reach the ship by following the long array of lights that stood out like stars in the blackness. Ed placed a hand on the hull of the great warship, like he wanted to determine if it was really there. Once satisfied, Ed looked up, cuffed his hands and shouted up into the air.

"Hallo!" Ed called up.

There was no answer.

"Hallo!" Ed yelled, much harder this time.

"Who's there?" called back an unseen voice.

"Four travellers," Ed shouted back. "We've come a long way. Dr. Kina told us to come here."

"Wait one moment!" the voice yelled, in return.

After several minutes, a rope ladder unravelled along the side of the *Pedigree*. "Come on up!" the voice called, as the rope ladder hit the hard ice.

One at a time, they made their way up. First Travis, then Alice and Zach, and finally Ed. Climbing proved to be an intimidating venture. As each person moved higher on the ladder, the ground below became more of a dark abyss. Alice watched as an enamel mug slipped from her backpack and fell. After what seemed like a few minutes, a shattering clang rang out.

At the top, their welcome was not what was expected. Several scruffy-looking crewmembers had Ed, Zach, Travis and Alice surrounded. Each sailor was armed with a gun and looked prepared to use it.

"Move aside, boys!" ordered a voice from behind the crew. A boar in blue slacks and a white shirt emerged from behind the crowd. "Ah! You mus' be Mr. Edward!" the boar cried, as he saw Ed and company. "We were hopin' you would get here soon." the captain then turned to his crew. "Drop yer guns, lads." he ordered. "These folks are expected."

Just then, Jolly Roger crashed in. "Hallo, all," the gull greeted, but no one seemed to take much notice.

As the crew returned to their posts, the boar led Alice, Ed, Travis and Zach to his quarters on the ship.

"Pleasure to meet you all," the boar said, at last. "Captain Joseph 'Jo' Mulligan at your service." The boar turned his attention to Zach to offer a trotter to shake. "It's a pleasure to meet you at last Mr. Edward."

"Good to see you, Mr. Mulligan," said Ed politely from the side. "These are my companions, Alice, Zach and Travis. We were coming along by sea to meet with your ship when we struck the ice bank."

"You lot go' off lucky," commented Mulligan, as he poured some hot water into enamel mugs of tea. "We got ourselves trapped in this ice when tha' bloo'y clou' landed. We tried breaking the ice with our cannons but that did nothin' except get us attacked by flyin' snakes all day since. We're sittin' duck 'ere."

Over the cup of hot tea, Ed provided the narrative of what had happened, making sure he gave everything he knew over to the sea captain.

"Wha' abou' the bird?" asked Mulligan, as he pointed at Jolly Roger when the account was finished.

"Oi!" snapped the gull. "I'll 'ave you know I'm 'ead of the Royal Army of Gulls and loyal servant to King Stormwing of the floating castle *Auld Lang Syne*."

"Don't worry about him," explained Ed. "He's the one who guided us to your ship."

"Righ'," grunted Mulligan. He didn't say much after that, just led them to a set of rooms adjacent to his own. "You are welcome to stay as long as you need to," Mulligan added, before leaving them.

The four were now alone. After setting the sleeping arrangements and grabbing a late supper of soup and some buttered bread from the ship's mess hall, everyone made their way to bed. Everyone except Ed and Zach. The two young men sat in the little common area that was located between the set of rooms.

Zach couldn't sleep, his mind was trying to take in all that had happened. First, Ed was dead, then it turned out he was alive and living in another world altogether. After that, there was the trip through the tunnel via fireplaces, and the trip to town. Then they were in Bathill, delivering a report to the Deltic government, warning the kingdom of the arrival of the Manookoo cloud. It seemed to Zach that he was in a dream, one that seemed confusing and without end.

Ed was deep in thought. He couldn't forgive himself for what had happened. In bringing his friends to the Gallan-Gallet, he had opened them up to the risk of death. For all Ed knew, Little Dill and his brownie army were shredded by the Manookoo. With Little Dill possibly gone and no way to possibly get help, Ed felt as if he would be powerless to stop what might happen to his friends. The fear made him feel ill as he looked out of one of the round windows onto the black abyss outside.

The next morning, Ed, Zach, Travis, and Alice were assigned jobs and flung into back-breaking work. Alice was sent below decks to help in refueling the *Pedigree's* dynamo, while Zach and Travis were sent to help move boxes in the stockroom. Every time a job was finished, a new one would pop up.

Ed was more fortunate. Mulligan allowed the young man to utilize the wireless system to notify Bloom and Kina that they had arrived and inform them of the events that occurred after their crash on the ice bed. He then proceeded to join the rest of the wireless crew in notifying other warships of the Manookoo's path, but proved to be so inexperienced that Mulligan sent him to help Alice with the dynamo.

Captain Jolly Roger was not exempt from work, either. Under Ed's orders, the seagull made his way to the wrecked boat to find Little Dill and any of the brownies. He set out at the first sign of light and promised to return before nightfall.

At noon, Ed and the others picnicked on the bridge. It was a modest meal of bread, cheese and some smoked meat the sailors called "musker," with some cold tea from that morning's breakfast to wash it down.

Ed, Travis, Zach and Alice were too caught up in their own thoughts to notice Jolly Roger fly in. The bird carried what looked like a rag of sorts with something cradled inside in his beak.

"'Ere, 'ere lads!" Jolly Roger called, in a muffled voice. "I 'ave a 'ur'ise 'or 'ou!"

It wasn't until the seagull crashed into the group that anyone noticed. The rag and the object inside landed on one of the empty plates. It was Little Dill, battered from the chaos of war. His uniform was torn and tattered, and a few stiches on his head were loosened, revealing some well-yellowed cotton.

"Hellos," the little toy said wearily, before stumbling backwards and landing on his bottom.

"It wasn't a pretty sight, lads," the bird explained in his usual way, as he sucked tea from an enamel cup. "There wasn't much left when I reached the boat. I found the wee lad among the wreckage."

"Wreckage?" Ed cried.

"They destroyed...everything," Little Dill replied, weakly. "No more boats..." It took some time before Little Dill had enough strength to tell of his fight. Ed placed the tired toy in his bunk while Jolly Roger explained the situation.

"Was there anyone else?" asked Alice, remembering the brownies.

"Not sure. I can make another trip in a while if ye like. Those monster things destroyed the boat. No supplies survived, from what I could see."

When Ed returned, Jolly Roger gave him the same report and then set out again for the wreck. The gull had promised he would be much faster now that he knew where the boat was and would return when he had finished his search.

Once the bird was gone, Ed and the others returned to their work. Mulligan relieved them of their duties for the day by dinner. It was not long after their meal that the sound of bugles could be heard across the horizon, getting louder and sharper by the minute. Not long after this, there was a great fuss made on the port side of the *Pedigree*. Mulligan was called to see to it, and after some shouting and cursing, he ran below decks to get Ed and the others. "You be'er ge' up 'ere," he snapped, before marching back upstairs.

When Ed, Alice, Zach, and Travis arrived, they were directed by Mulligan to the port edge where a spotlight had been set. Looking down below, they were surprised to see a very unimpressed Bug-a-Boo standing on a boat made from random pieces of scrap wood that seemed to build up at the stern into a boxy tower. Ed couldn't help but wonder how it was able to cross the ice field.

"Ed!" Bug-a-Boo bellowed from below. "Will you tell this accursed sea urchin that I mean no harm and to let me board?"

"I told you I can't let you on," Mulligan snapped back, "unless you tell us who you are!"

"And I've already told you who I am! Doctor Cosmo Maximilian Bug-a-Palooza-Pick-a-Low-Boo, Doctorate in charms and spells, High Warden for the Realm of the North, and chief clerk for the Order of the Four Keepers."

"You can trust him with that," assured Ed.

Mulligan made a sigh. "Right boys," he said at last. "Let down the ladder."

The whole group jumped back in surprise when up from hatches at either end of the patchwork boat flew two flocks of birds. First came a few eagles wearing iron helmets and breastplates and carrying heavy spears in their talons. Following them were some pigeons with golden broaches tied around their necks and black caps upon their heads. When the pigeons landed on deck, one of them cried in a low and clear voice: "His Majesty King Stormwing, King of the Periculosus Ocean, Ward of the Foam Hills of Nimbus, Duke of the Pearl Coast and Prince Regent of Bird Island!" When this announcement was made, up from the black abyss came a pelican, dressed as royally as possible with a gold chain with various ribbons and bits of sea rock hanging from his neck and a crown made from dead coral atop of his head. Following the regal pelican was Bug-a-Boo, looking extremely unpleased and tired from climbing up the rope ladder and pulling himself up onto the ship, landing on his side with a hard thud as he climbed over the lip of the ship onto the deck.

"That's the last time I get help from birds," grumbled the wizard and he pulled himself up.

While Mulligan was stuck talking to King Stormwing, Bug-a-Boo had a meeting with Ed, Travis, Zach and Alice in the quartet's rooms.

"When the radio went out," Bug-a-Boo explained, "I rushed here as quick as I could to see that you lot were all right."

"You took longer than you should have," commented Travis.

"I would have used my pipe," the wizard defended, "but I made it as far as Stormwing's castle. I can only conclude that Horcus designed Spyrus to withstand charms."

"How *charming*," Ed said, humorously.

"This is not a time for trivial puns, Ed," Bug-a-Boo snapped back. "Out there, a vengeful demi-god is moving toward your home. Anyways, I was fortunate enough to run into Stormwing, who owed me a favour from a while back and agreed to bring me here. When we ran into the cloud, his eagle guards were quick enough to lift the boat…castle, whatever you call it, on top of the ice. It was after this that we saw your gull, he directed us to the *Pedigree* and went the opposite direction, something about survivors, if I remember correctly."

At that moment, Little Dill stirred from his sleep on a makeshift bed.

"What have we here," Bug-a-Boo said, as he scooped Little Dill into his hands.

Little Dill just gave an innocent look.

"Such a mess, too," the wizard continued. "An antique should never go into battle. Alice, see if there is a needle and thread about, I won't have this toy go out in such a state."

It did not take Bug-a-Boo long to sew up Little Dill's torn stitches. Once the wizard had finished his work, Little Dill gave his account of the battle. There wasn't much to tell, except that Little Dill and the brownies only just barely won their fight against the creatures. When the toy finished his narrative, it was Bug-a-Boo's turn.

"I have some disturbing developments to tell you," he explained. "It appears Manoo will be more dangerous than we thought. From what my research tells me, Manoo is not just a god, but a titan as well."

"That couldn't be any worse," put in Zach.

"Well, young man, titans can be unpredictable," Bug-a-Boo interrupted, starting to lose patience.

"Like wizards?" Zach mocked.

"Especially like wizards."

Bug-a-Boo went on: "There was a time when they dwelled in this world but were killed off during the Campaign of the Faerie."

"The wha'?"

"It was a battle so great that only myth could contain it. When the Faerie King Gregon grew tired of the power the titans held over all creation, he led an army against Clawfoot the Destroyer, king of the titans. According to myth, it lasted three hundred years and led to the end of the rule of the titans and the rise of the current age, the Faerie Age. The only ones that did survive were the lesser beings that make up what we know as giants. From what I found in the records house in Nimbus, it is said that Horcus fell in love with a titan named Ironbone and it was she who bore Manoo. There isn't very much to know after that. We know Manoo became the god of the dead, then betrayed Horcus by siding with the Manookoo over human sacrificing and was thus locked away on Spyrus."

"But none of the myths mention anything about him being a titan." Ed protested.

"That is true," Bug-a-boo replied, "but upon studying the original sources, I was able to realize a slight error on the part of the translators. The word *gigo*[19] is used interchangeably to mean giant and titan in the texts. Seeing as Manoo was the son of a titan, it

---

[19] Pronounced: Guy/gō

is logical that he would be one, especially considering he inherited his father's godly powers."

The room became quiet as Bug-a-Boo pulled on his pipe. Blue smoke frothed out from it sleepily.

"Does he have a weakness?" asked Ed. "I mean *all* the Zeltic gods had a weakness."

Bug-a-Boo perked up at this. "There was one," he said, "but it's quite a challenge and I'm only going on a hunch."

"Well, what is it?"

"Spyrus, according to the *Great Tome of Bartleby*, was created using part of Manoo's soul so he would be neither living nor dead. It would have been marked on Spyrus with a seal, so if Horcus felt it necessary Manoo could be easily killed off."

"I thought you couldn't kill a god," commented Alice.

"Not in this case, my dear," replied Bug-a-Boo, as he lay down his pipe. "As Manoo is half a god, he is not granted the power of pure immortality. This means he is open for an attack, but since part of him is trapped in Spyrus, he is protected unless the seal is broken. Besides, Zeltic gods may be able to live forever, but that doesn't mean they can't be killed. Death comes for all things eventually, in this world."

"So, the only solution is to go further up and further in. But then where do we find it? The cloud has spread itself over several leagues. It'll be like looking for a needle in a purple haystack," Ed added

"Oh! oh! I gots it!" cried Little Dill, enthusiastically.

"Well, what is it then?" inquired Bug-a-Boo, impatiently.

"We knows the clouds is movings, rights?"

Everyone nodded.

"So, logic-co-co-ly we just has to wait."

"Seems a bit of a risk," commented Zach.

"Whats do yous gots?" snapped Little Dill.

"Our little friend is right," murmured Bug-a-Boo. "Spyrus is on the move but waiting contains a variety of unknown possibilities and can take up quite a bit of time, a resource we do not have."

Little Dill piped up again, this time determined to not let his idea go unheard and dismissed by Bug-a-Boo. "Why don'ts we use the birdies then?" the little doll said, jumping up and down to attract attention and pointing at Stormwing, who had chosen to sit in on the meeting.

"I beg your pardon?" the bird king snapped.

"Not you, of course, Your Grace," said Bug-a-Boo, trying to soothe the bird king's feelings.

"I can spare a few soldiers," Stormwing said, "but I refuse to risk any of my officers to lead the search."

"Oh! oh! Pick me! Pick me!" Little Dill cried, still jumping.

Stormwing began to laugh. "Why would I choose you?" the bird king snorted.

"'Cause I've beens t'rough more wars than yous could shakes a stick at!" Little Dill snapped back, with a stern glare.

Stormwing was taken aback. He had never had someone—let alone a toy—snap back at him before.

The following morning, the *Pedigree* was abuzz with action. Above decks, Mulligan and his crew were picking off any Manoo creatures that flew overhead. At the same time, Little Dill, who had been dubbed colonel-in-chief of the search party, was making plans with Jolly Roger, who had only just returned that morning with what was left of the brownies from the wreck.

Below decks, things were not as hectic. Travis and Alice were planning the supplies they would need for their part of the trip while Ed and Zach helped Bug-a-Boo with the preparation of charms, though the wizard doubted they would be of much use.

Before leaving, Little Dill came below to say goodbye. He looked smart in the uniform one of the pigeons made for him, with a medal from Stormwing to commemorate his appointment. "Mark the words on it well," the King bird noted, "it has the sacred motto of my family upon it."

"Whats is it?" asked Little Dill.

Stormwing squawked something in pelican and then returned to speaking in English: "'Charge forth and carry what is sacred.' I hope you will follow these words, little warrior."

Little Dill blushed, but quickly covered it with a stiff salute and climbed on board Jolly Roger. The two flew off, leading the army of eagles to find Spyrus.

Chapter X
The March on Spyrus

High in the skies, Little Dill searched for the rock Spyrus on the back of Captain Jolly Roger. From a pair of oversize binoculars, the little toy looked, but there was no sign of the rock. Behind the pair were an army of one hundred eagles, each dressed with breastplate armour and armed with pointed spears in their talons to fight against the Manookoo monsters in the event of an attack.

"Any sign of the rock?" asked Jolly Roger.

"Nots yet!" Little Dill called back.

The flock steered to the left. Nothing. To the right. Still nothing. All they could see was purple mist flowing everywhere.

Jolly Roger dived down, the eagles following suit. Soon their bellies were an inch from the ice as they glided over the surface. Just as fast as they were below, they rose back up again and veered west. The sudden turn caused Little Dill's hat to be flung from his head and fall into the violet abyss.

"We're losing light, sir," called one from the eagles, from behind.

Little Dill wasn't listening though, he was too absorbed in looking for Spyrus.

"He's quite right!" Jolly Roger called back. "We'll have no way of getting back if we don't leave now while the sun is still out."

Little Dill heard the seagull this time and reluctantly agreed to travel back to the *Pedigree*. The flock was about to turn around when from their right came a crowd of flying deformed snake-like creatures. Jolly Roger dove down to avoid them while the eagles charged head-on into the oncoming mass.

Jolly Roger surged left and right as eagles and monsters fell from the sky, landing on the hard ice below. Both toy and bird knew that there was little chance of going back while the conflict above them was in process but sitting and waiting would not be a wise choice, either. The best option Jolly Roger could come up with was to keep moving as much as possible and avoid being noticed by the Manookoo.

Left and right. Up and down. Over and under.

Little Dill gripped tightly to the seagull with all his might, hoping not to be knocked off. There was little hope that they would make it out alive now.

Jolly Roger was losing strength, he needed a chance to rest before they could even try to make it back to the ship. In the distance there was what looked like a blackish mass, large and round. The pair didn't notice that it was the mass that the Manookoo were streaming from, nor would they have cared if they had.

Jolly Roger just made it to the shore (if that is even the right word for it) and rested on the smooth slopped surface. From there, Little Dill and Jolly Roger could both see the fighting. The eagles had a slight advantage, but the Manookoo creatures were starting to gain the upper hand. Little Dill looked at Jolly Roger.

Jolly Roger looked back at Little Dill. In a moment it soon occurred to them.

"I do believe," the bird concluded, "we have found that rock Spyrus after all."

"It is! It is!" the little toy cried back, jumping with glee.

"We have to get back to the ship," Jolly Roger realized. "We need to tell Ed an' them about our find."

"But hows? Those snakey t'ings ares all overs the places."

"Right," said the bird. "I guess we'll just have to charge through and hope for the best. Get back on my back. Hang on tight. I wasn't named captain for nothing."

With a run, a jump and the flap of a wing, Jolly Roger was soon gliding close to the ice field. Whenever an enemy or an ally fell from the battle in the sky, the seagull would veer to avoid collision. Little Dill tried to signal as many of the eagles as he could of the sudden retreat, trying his hardest not to lose his grip on his flying friend. Some of the eagles stayed behind to hold off the snake-creatures, so those who were growing tired could retreat with Little Dill and Jolly Roger.

Ed and Travis were on the bridge with Captain Mulligan, looking over a map of the Periculosus Sea and the Gallan-Gallet, marking where the cloud was currently moving so they could estimate the time before it would reach the island.

"They've got a day 'er two at most," Mulligan said, solemnly, "bu' my bes' guess is it'll reach the coast by morning and then make its way across. Any ground forces are going to need to be ready." The captain then scribbled on a sheet of paper and handed it to one of the crewmembers.

"What I'm interested in knowing," added Ed, "is where on earth Spyrus is hiding. By the way the reports of its movement, you would think that it would be up, leading the cloud; but when we hit the ice field there was no evidence of it even there."

"Unless your little friend and tha' bird get back 'ere in one piece," Mulligan answered, pessimistically, "we're up t'e creek wit'ou' a pa'le."

There came a moment of silence. Suddenly, a faint call came from the distance. The three looked up to see Little Dill and Jolly Roger flying back to the ship. With a crash into the table, toy and bird made it back in one piece, with the remaining eagles following suit. Many were tired and somewhat battered from the conflict. Mulligan ordered the infirmary to be opened for the eagles while an emergency meeting was held on the bridge.

Little Dill told everyone what he and Jolly Roger had seen on their expedition.

"Our bow is pointed west, so that means our rock is headin' from the stern eastward to the Forestlands," Mulligan observed, looking at the map. "That puts it roughly south of here by approximately fifteen to thirty leagues. We're gonna need to act fast."

"That's gonna be easier said than done," Zach added, pointing at the direction Mulligan had been referring too. "If we're going that way, there's a good chance those snake creatures are going to attack. We know they're defending Spyrus since they went after Little Dill and Roger once they got close. I'm not saying we can't do it; I'm saying we're going to need cover when we go."

"We still have the brownies," Ed answered.

"But how long will they hold?"

"I don't know."

"Then forget them. We're going to need something to keep those things at bay."

"Then what do you suggest?" Ed asked, hotly. "Seems like you want to criticize but not give a solution."

"I am," Zach fired back. "I just don't like following a dumb idea."

"Then give a better one!"

"Easy," Alice interrupted. "We can still use the Brownies, but we'll just need something to back 'em up."

"I will provide some more of my guard to support your venture," Stormwing offered.

"Well, that's settled," said Bug-a-Boo, as he pulled from his pipe. "Now, I suppose I ought to list out what we know. First, the Zeltic demi-god Manoo is locked up with his cult in a floating rock. Second, said rock is shrouded in a thick purple fog that is bent on destroying the Deltic Empire. Third, the only known weakness of Manoo is to break the seal that is keeping said rock in existence."

"Well," answered Travis, "we at least know what we need to do."

"I hope you all know," Bug-a-Boo went on, solemnly, "this is going to be very dangerous. Manoo will be relentless and there is no knowing what he'll be doing when we get there. As a titan, he has the power to do, and will do, whatever he can to squash his enemies."

"Yes," Ed answered.

"Good. It helps to know what you're getting into before doing something stupid."

The next morning, everyone was ready for battle. One of the *Pedigree's* lifeboats was modified to act as a sled to get Bug-a-Boo, Ed, Travis, Zach and Alice across the frozen ocean to Spyrus, and they made harnesses out of rope to be worn by some of Stormwing's eagles.

It was midday once everyone was ready. Through the purple haze was a vague abyss that showed nothing of their destination. The sled was pointed roughly in the direction Little Dill and the search party had traveled the day before. After a few goodbyes and well-wishes, the eagle-driven sled containing the four young adults and a wizard set out along the ice. Ahead of the group was a small convocation of eagles who would act as protection should they run into trouble, and Little Dill and Jolly Roger acting as guides, though it was advised that the pair should flee to the sled if they ran into any of those flying snake-creatures again. Captain Mulligan insisted they wait until morning to set out, but Ed disagreed. He thought they needed to head out as soon as possible before they lost track of the floating rock.

As the sled bolted into the purple haze, Alice looked back on the *Pedigree* and watched as the old, ironclad ship grew smaller and faded into the mist. It was hard to see Little Dill through the haze; everyone could barely make out Jolly Roger for a few moments before he was lost in the mist.

The journey was an uncomfortable one. The frozen saltwater had been captured in mid-wave at some points, causing the boat to jump every so often as it sped along. Despite the sky being hard to see, a heavy rain fell on the small band. The only protection they could find was an old canvas tarp that had been left in the boat.

Eventually, Jolly Roger and Little Dill flew back down to the sled, the two were soaked from the rain but didn't seem much bothered by the ordeal.

"We're almost there!" Little Dill cried.

"Some of the eagles saw some of those Manoo creatures ahead," Jolly Roger explained. "They're going to stage a distraction for us, so we can get on through. We should be at Spyrus shortly."

At that moment, there came the squeal of a beast in great pain and the sound of metal clanging.

"There they go," observed Ed.

"No time for that," interrupted Bug-a-Boo. "Look!"

There before them was the rock Spyrus, moving ominously at a slow pace across the ice sheet. Even through the purple fog, everyone could see it.

Chapter XI
The Trial of Horcus

~*~

Jolly Roger flew up to the eagles that were pulling the sled and informed them of what was to be done next. The eagles began to adjust their course, so they could transfer onto the rock.

Getting onto the monolith wasn't hard. The eagles needed to only fly close enough as to allow the sled to slide up onto the shore of Spyrus. Despite Spyrus' movement, walking was quite easy.

"Right," whispered Bug-a-Boo. "Now that we're here, we need to be on our guard while we look for the seal."

"Do we even know what it looks like?" Zach put in. "I feel like this was never really specified."

"Zach's got a point," Ed said.

"That's because we don't know what it looks like," Bug-a-Boo replied. "It was hard enough figuring out if there was some sort of seal, much less what it looks like."

"Maybe we should split up," suggested Travis. "It's too big for us to all go it together and it won't make a difference if we don't know what it looks like."

"Even Travis has one," Ed commented. "Normally he gets only one of those a week."

Travis gave Ed a look.

"I don't want to risk it," Bug-a-Boo went on, pausing for a second. "No. It isn't right. There's a good chance we'll find the seal with Manoo if we stick together."

With the old wizard getting the final word on the matter, everyone began the trek along Spyrus. The eagles stayed behind to keep watch and to provide an easy escape when the time came.

The surface of Spyrus was quite smooth and the steeper areas were noticeably harder to climb. The fog didn't make it any easier, with some craters being hidden by random, thick gobs of the fog. At one point, Travis nearly fell into one of the craters.

"Careful!" Zach cried, as he caught Travis. "Last thing we need is a casualty."

Not long after that, everyone decided to set up camp for the night.

"There's not much point in going any further," Ed argued. "It's hard enough to walk in this fog without someone breaking their neck, the dark'll just make it worse."

They were too exposed on the surface for a proper fire and had to rely on a small mound of coals for warmth.

Into the Faerie Lands

For extra protection, everyone took turns keeping watch through the night, which wasn't the worst thing as they had Little Dill to keep them company, since the small toy didn't need to sleep.

In the morning they started out again. This time, Jolly Roger flew a bit ahead to see if there was anything important. Occasionally, the seagull would return to warn them of some craters, and then fly back. The day ended with another fireless campout and no results.

The next morning began with more hiking before stopping for a brief luncheon. Bug-a-Boo kept lamenting about the situation as he fingered through a small book of notes.

"Wha's up, Ed?" Zach inquired, noticing a quizzical expression on his friend's face.

"Do you hear something?" Ed asked. "Like heavy breathing."

"I don't hear anything," said Travis.

"I'm hearin' something," Ed insisted.

From one of the craters a few miles away, fire shot out into the air.

"I think we found our titan," Ed chuntered, and jumped to his feet.

Jolly Roger flew ahead to scout for any danger and was quick to return with an "all clear" report.

When everyone arrived at the cave, they were met with the smell of decay and burning. Alice poked her head over the opening when she heard something big and hot coming up the cavern. Alice was just fast enough to pull away in time.

Swoo-oosh! went a geyser of flames into the air. It lasted for a few minutes and then dissipated.

"Something's down there, that's for sure," agreed Bug-a-Boo.

"Could it lead to Manoo?" asked Alice.

"Possibly," Ed answered. "The only problem is that fire."

Zach looked at his watch, his lips moving like he was counting. "Fifty-five, fifty-six, fifty-seven…" he counted. "Two minutes. One, two, three…" and so on and so forth until another flaming geyser shot up.

"Ten minutes!" Zach announced.

"What about ten minutes?" asked Ed.

"That's how much time we've got before the next flame shoots up."

"You don't honestly think there's a way down there?" doubted Bug-a-Boo.

"Have you any other ideas?" Zach shot.

"Yes. We keep going. There's no guarantee that this cavern goes anywhere."

"The longer we wander, the more likely it is that this rock has made landfall."

"You're being too careless about this, Zacchaeus. If we go down that way, there's no knowing how long we'd have before we'd find an opening. We are far more likely to be roasted down there."

The tense argument was soon broken by another blast of fire.

"There goes another ten minutes," Travis muttered to Ed and Alice.

Jolly Roger and Little Dill were losing patience. As soon as the fire stopped, the bird and toy set out down the cavern. They made it back just before the flames shot up.

"There's a cave down there," Jolly Roger explained. "Could easily get to it if we're fast enough."

"So, there's a cave," Ed pondered. "Could lead to Manoo, could not."

"I'm starting to wonder if the fire is even real," Alice put in.

"What do you mean?"

"Haven't you noticed that there's no heat from the fire when it shoots out?"

"Now that you mention it," added Bug-a-Boo, "it's not hot at all."

"So, it has to be an illusion," concluded Travis.

"Bingo," said Ed. "We just need to make sure that it's true and not a real trap."

"I'll doos it!" piped Little Dill, and he started puttering to the edge of the crater. "If you guys are goings to arg'oo 'bouts it, I mights as wells."

Before anyone could do anything, a rush of flame erupted into the air. Everyone watched in horror as Little Dill leaned over the edge and the flames rushed past him.

Nothing happened.

"Obviously a trick," observed Zach.

"Could have been Horus' way of keeping intruders out," Ed added. "I remember George telling me once that Horcus was always a paranoid god. There's a good chance that this won't be the last trick to keep intruders out."

"Great," fumed Zach, "a god with a paranoia complex. What next? One with a Napoleon complex or Freudian issues?"

"Now is not the time for quips," Bug-a-Boo interrupted. "Now that we know that it is safe to go in, we may as well prepare ourselves for what's to come."

When the flames died down, Ed and Travis peered down into the pit. It seemed to go downward and then curve into a horizontal position. There was no sign of any flame to light the way below, further confirming that the flaming geyser was just an illusion.

Using some pegs and rope, everyone made their way down to the bottom of the cavern, still feeling uneasy whenever the flames would shoot up. Little Dill, however, rode on Jolly Roger and met everyone at the bottom quite quickly.

"Tooks yous long enough!" the little doll mocked, as everyone finally reached the bottom.

They left the rope behind as the group began to make their way through the tunnel with lamps. The long cavern curved in every direction, making it hard to determine whether they were going the right way at times. It was eerily quiet; the only sound was their feet tapping along the solid stone.

"We should be getting close," said Bug-a-Boo, trying not to be too loud.

"What makes you so sure?" Zach quizzed.

"A tunnel can't go on forever, young man. Eventually, we should find the end."

"Oi!" Ed called. "I think there's an opening ahead."

"How can you tell?" asked Travis. "It's so dark here, I can barely see my hand in front of my face."

"I can hear the wind," Ed replied. "I know it sounds weird but if you listen closely, you can hear the wind whizzing across the opening."

Zach lifted his lamp to reveal in the black void a set of stone steps leading up to what looked like a decayed wooden trapdoor. Because of its age, several cracks and gaps where the wood had broken and rotted allowed for air to seep through it from the chamber above into the shaft.

Alice approached the trapdoor cautiously. She could hear the slight sound of the wind—Ed was quite right about that—but it was hard to tell what was above due to it being so dark. She tried to push the hatch but it started to crumble as she pushed and in the end Alice was forced to retreat to the others as the door fell from its place.

Jolly Roger fluttered up to the opening with a lamp clutched in his talons. The little light seemed to float for a few seconds as the gull went up and then disappeared.

Everyone waited in anticipation. In the few moments they waited, time stretched into what felt like an eternity.

At last, Jolly Roger returned.

"There's something up there, alright," he replied. "Not sure what. There was an odd sound."

"What sort of sound?" Ed asked.

"Like somethin' large was breathin'."

Chapter XII
The Lone Titan

It took a few minutes for everyone to climb, but once they were up Ed, Zach, Travis, Alice, Bug-a-Boo, Little Dill and Jolly Roger could easily see what was before them. The new area was vast, with rows of torches burning for miles and illuminating a white marble floor. In the middle was a massive stone block serving as an altar with runes inscribed all over it and dried blood on the top, while a foul smell of incense hung in the air.

Everyone approached the stone, it smelled of decay and seemed to be the only thing that could overpower the incense. Bug-a-Boo surveyed the runes on the alter.

"What does it say?" Travis asked.

"'Here are the damned,'" read Bug-a-Boo. "'Given up in the name of Father Horcus for the forgiveness of the Lone Titan.'"

"Must be where Manoo's minions take their victims," commented Ed. "The whole place reeks of death."

"There's more life than death here little man," hissed a voice from the black shadows.

"Who's there!?" cried Alice.

"I am everywhere and nowhere," the voice taunted. "I am dual. I am multiple. I am one. Some call me the Lone Titan, others the Bastard of Horcus."

Everything seemed to happen at once. Out of the shadows came a snake-like creature: head of a snake, torso of a man, and the lower half, the body of a snake. The torso was dressed in ancient armour and was wielding a large battle axe in both its hands. The creature charged at Ed, axe poised, ready to strike. Ed tried to jump to the right to avoid the attack but was struck by the edge of the axe and collided with Zach, together they hit the hard marble floor and crashed into one of the torches.

The creature recoiled, ready for another strike. Zach, still in pain from the collision, attempted to hurl a hunk of burning wood at the monster. With luck, it hit the creature, but the scaly brute was still attracted by the others. It was about to pounce again when a large hand from the dark appeared and grabbed the creature.

"That is enough," the same voice hissed as the hand gripped the monster.

"Who is this!?" called Bug-a-Boo.

Alice and Travis ran over to Ed and Zach. Both were hurt badly from the attack. Zach's shoulder was scratched and bruised, and he had a gash across the back of his head. Ed's face was badly cut; his left eye not even spared from the assault. Alice and Travis wasted no time bandaging their injured friends.

Out of a heavily-shadowed end of the room appeared a big head with a handsome face and a nattered mess of long black hair.

"It is I, Manoo," the face replied. "Damned to live my days on this rock they call Spyrus."

Bug-a-Boo produced from his coat a sapphire orb and proceeded to shake it. The orb began to glow, Bug-a-Boo let go of it, and it floated up high above everyone. The orb let out such a radiant glow that it illuminated the entire room. It was then that everyone could behold Manoo, the titanic child of Horcus and the titan Ironbone.

Manoo was a massive titan, over one hundred feet in height and dressed in rags, with chains and fetters latched around his arms, legs and neck. His body was riddled with patches of snake scales and the right side of his torso was fused to the wall.

"Who dares disturb me in my slumber?" the titan boomed.

Bug-a-Boo gave a curt bow and introduced himself and the others. The titan hurled the snake creature across the room and leaned in as best he could to take a closer look at them. In the meantime, Ed and Zach were able to gather enough strength to stand.

"I apologise for the reaction of Temor," Manoo atoned. "He is my guard and sent to prevent anyone from breaking my soul."

Manoo pointed to the rune-and-blood-covered altar.

"So that is how Horcus has kept you trapped," Ed commented.

"The story of my sealing has been wrapped in a lie of rebellion on myself and my worshipers," Manoo explained, and told his long tale: "Long ago, before time eternal, the first gods, Void and Naught, fashioned the universe by taming dragons and locking them in spheres. Unsure of what to do with these creations, the two fought and Void slayed Naught. Horrified by his sin, Void went into a long sleep that will only end when time is over, and then he will destroy all creation to revive Naught.

"From Naught's blood came the oceans, his flesh became sand and soil, his hair became all the flora, his teeth the twenty-four gods of the Zeltic and the marrow of his bones became all the creatures of creation. From the bones came the first masters of the world, the titans. They believed the world was their birthright and enslaved all creation, forcing it to their bidding. For forty thousand years, the titans ruled like gods and worshiped the twenty-four gods as thanks for this right, holding Horcus as the highest of them all. The gods, in their gratitude, turned a blind eye to the cruelty the titans executed on the world.

"Eventually, humanity and the Fae became tired of their gigantic overlords and rebelled. Among this rebellious group was a cult who sacrificed all that were captured as tribute so that they may defeat the titans. Horcus became enraged and wanted to destroy this cult. Things did not become better when the tide of the war turned against him. So, Horcus intended to wake Void and bring about the destruction of the universe so that he would win, even if it meant becoming a tooth. I objected and helped the cult, now called Manookoo, attack Horcus.

"In the long fight, Horcus cursed me and my followers to this rock. Now I must spend my days feeding on the flesh of innocents who are made to appear as sinners of unknown crimes. What I would give for this fate to be over! Alas, I am forced to stay and rot in this tomb."

"There may be a way," Bug-a-Boo replied, and he explained about the sealing of Manoo's soul to the rock.

"The only thing I know that has the seal of my father on it would be on the altar," said the titan, and proceeded to reach with a mighty fist to destroy it. As the fist became close, a flash of white light crackled from the altar and the fist flew back.

"Of course," Ed mumbled, weakly. "The seal can't be broken that easily. Horcus probably knew that would happen eventually."

Everyone examined the altar. In raised letters and covered in blood on its top was a large rune in the middle of a twenty-four-pointed star, an ideogram, made up of a series of intricate runes.

"'Only my breath can break this curse,'" Bug-a-boo read, from the runes.

"I doubt Horcus would want us to shout, 'be gone,' or something like that," Zach added.

Little Dill jumped on top of the altar and began to blow on it, taking deep heaving breaths and blowing as hard as he could.

"It's no use," Bug-a-Boo said, as he picked up the small toy and placed him on the floor. "This is far more complicated."

Little Dill was having none of it. He jumped up and down trying to get everyone's attention for another idea but was ordered by Bug-a-Boo to stand aside and wait. Annoyed, Little Dill ran up to Jolly Roger and began to whisper something into the seagull's ear. Roger nodded, Little Dill jumped on Roger's back, and the two flew over to some of the burning broken torches. The seagull gripped one by the safe end and carried it to the altar.

"Tries this!" Little Dill cried.

"It's worth a try," Jolly Roger argued. "At worse, nothing happens."

Bug-a-Boo let out a hard sigh and reluctantly agreed.

Jolly Roger dropped the flaming wood on the altar. The flame burned for a short while until it died out and the wood became only red embers and black ash.

In seconds the blood-covered surface began to burn, smoldering at first, then yellow and blue flames began to lick the air and spread across the altar until the flames burst into a mighty combustion that put out the rest of the torches.

When the smoke and drama had died, the only light in the space was the glowing orb. The orb slowly floated down to Bug-a-Boo. The altar was only rubble and the torches now just poles of wood with charred tips. Manoo crawled forward, everyone could see that his skin was free of scales and no longer attached to the walls of the rock.

"Thank you," the titan said. "It has been a long time since I could breathe air freely and feel the sun upon me. I shall not take this gift you have given me for granted."

"You'll have a very different world to see once you leave here," called Bug-a-Boo, from below.

"That is something I look forward to," Manoo replied.

From the far end of the cavern, there came a sudden gust of fresh air and light from outside as two large stones slid away. Beyond, everyone could see blue sky and ocean with not a speck of purple fog to be seen across the horizon. Several leagues away, the faint green and white shores of the Crown Island of the Gallan-Gallet could be seen in the distance.

"It's beautiful," Manoo observed, as tears rolled from his eyes.

Everyone agreed.

Manoo crawled toward the opening. He didn't flinch away from the light, the great titan only closed his eyes and let the sun's light wax across his face.

There came a rumbling, the ceiling began to quake and slide down. Manoo quickly braced himself against the ceiling and pushed against it with all his might.

"I should have expected my father wouldn't want me to leave here," Manoo commented and he grunted and struggled with the massive stone ceiling.

Everyone looked up at the titan.

"Go!" Manoo ordered. "My time was over ages ago!"

Ed, Zach, Travis, Alice, Bug-a-Boo, Little Dill and Jolly Roger ran for the opening. Pulling up before them were the eagles and the boat-sled—now more boat than sled! Everyone ran, water from the opening slowly flooding the room and reaching their knees as they got to the boat.

The eagles flapped their wings as hard as they could to ensure there was enough distance between them and the monolith.

There came a cry of pain from inside Spyrus, followed by a force of air escaping from the opening. The sudden gust took and eagles and the septet by surprise as they began to lose control. Spyrus began to draw more water into its mouth, pulling the boat and eagles in with it. The eagles tried to move fast and fight the new challenge, but the ropes snapped, pulling the boat back toward the rock and the eagles surging helplessly way.

Just as everyone thought they were going to be sucked back into Spyrus, the top lip of the opening smacked into the sea, causing a massive wave to torpedo the vessel away.

Everyone gripped tightly as the boat buffeted the waves; soon they were able to steady their dingy, and it drifted for a fair distance before slowing into a near stop. The party watched as the last of the great rock Spyrus sank into the ocean, leaving white-capped waves in its wake.

"So falls a once great and mighty god," Ed said, in awe.

"There are no gods, Ed," Bug-a-Boo added. "Just powerful beings who buy into their powers. Horcus thought he was able to keep humanity under the thumb of the titans and in the end, he and his kind are now but myths of the past while Manoo remains trapped in Spyrus."

"No," Zach said calmly. "I think he's finally free."

No more was said as there suddenly arose the sound of a faint whistle. Everyone looked back to see the *Pedigree* charging along the sapphire waters with black smoke billowing from her funnels and white foam slashing away from the bow.

Little Dill jumped upon Jolly Roger's back and flew over to the ship. It wasn't very long before *Pedigree* had changed her direction for the small boat.

"Thank the gods you lot are alive!" Captain Mulligan cried, as he greeted Ed, Alice, Travis and Bug-a-Boo back onboard the warship.

Jolly Roger looked about him. "Where is His Majesty?"

"Stormwing and his cronies high-tailed it when the fog and ice cleared," Mulligan explained. "I was told to let you know tha' you are to return to t'e castle at once. His Majesty wants to thank you personally."

The seagull made a curt salute and turned to the others. "I guess this is goodbye for now, then," Jolly Roger said.

"Just remember to stop by, Captain," Alice replied.

"Oh, I jolly well will, time permitting, of course!"

With that, Jolly Roger flapped his wings and set off in search of Stormwing's castle. When the seagull was out of sight, Captain Mulligan turned his attention to his crew. "Right lads!" he called. "Full steam for Bathill, there's no point gawking at a seagull all day!"

Chapter XIII
Making Things Done

~*~

At once, Mulligan had the weary travelers examined in the ship's infirmary. It wasn't long before Ed and Zach were covered in bandages while the ship doctor examined the injured pair.

"You'll need surgery on that eye," the ships doctor concluded as she examined Ed. "I can apply some balm to prevent corruption but the sooner it can be properly treated, the better your chances of keeping it."

"I suppose, I'm good to go." Zach assumed.

"Hardly," the doctor replied sternly, "your back will need stitching and that gash on the back of your head will be in need of cleaning before it develops corruption. The two of you will need to rest until we get to Bathill for proper examination."

"Why can't you treat us here?" asked Zach confusedly.

"Because we haven't any supplies left to do complicated treatments. For now, I can have you two temporarily bandaged, but once home you both can be properly examined."

They were never lonely; Alice, Travis, and Bug-a-boo came to visit them and keep them company. After a few days of bed rest, the doctor allowed Zach and Ed to go above deck to get some fresh are and sunlight.

When the *Pedigree* reached the mouth of the Dunbar River, Mulligan invited the weary heroes to a banquet in the ships mess to celebrate reaching home. It was at this point that Bug-a-boo needed to make his excuses.

"I'd stay longer," the wizard explained, "but I must go and report to Kina on what's transpired."

"Will we see you again?" asked Alice.

"Of course," was the reply, "how else are three getting home?"

With that, Bug-a-boo placed his pipe to mouth and the smoke from the bowl consumed him. When the smoke cleared, he was gone.

After a few days traveling along the Dunbar River, they were delivered to Bathill where Bloom arranged for everyone to be taken to a nearby hospital to be looked over. Ed was rushed off to surgery for the gash on his face while Zach was easily stitched and bandaged. Zach seemed to have no problems with being fussed over by the nurses, especially when he found himself attracted to one of the younger lady nurses who needed to draw blood for a sample. Travis and Alice were also examined but were deemed to be in good shape.

As a thank-you for their efforts, Bloom, under recommendation of parliament, arranged for private rooms at the hospital so Zach, Alice, and Travis could be near Ed for the moment he was finished being treated.

"When you are all better, I think you should stay with my wife and me at our apartments in the city," Bloom insisted. "Her Majesty would like to have an audience with you as thanks for your efforts."

Zach let out a snort, he had no time for monarchs and the like and would be none too happier for Ed to be out of surgery to take them back to Newtown.

"Both Her Majesty and the Lord Chancellor agree that you have all earned an Order of the Deltic Empire," Bloom went on, "for services in the protection of the Empire."

There came a knock at the door and a nurse entered the room.

"Mr. Worsley is ready to accept visitors," the nurse said, curtly.

Bloom stepped forward.

"He asked specifically for you three," the nurse added, gesturing toward Zach, Alice and Travis.

The nurse led the trio down the whitewashed hall to a corridor, and then up a flight of stairs to another corridor and another whitewashed hall. The nurse stopped at a door and entered alone; after a few seconds her head appeared from a crack. "He is ready for you now," was the announcement.

Everyone found Ed in a hospital bed looking haggard. Half his face was covered in a white bandage with a pad of cotton on his left eye.

"Well," announced Zach, "we'll have to call you *Danger Mouse* from now on."

Ed didn't seem to crack a smile.

"This is all my fault," Ed croaked, looking evermore in pain from his wounds.

"I don't know what you're talking about," Zach replied. "No one died…Well, besides Manoo, those who fought outside—"

Zach was cut off by a powerful elbow to the stomach by Alice.

"Ed," Travis said, "you've done nothing wrong. You warned everyone when something was going to happen, and we all saved the day."

Ed let out a weak smile. "Thanks," Ed replied, and then lifted his left hand to gesture toward his bandaged eye. "They had to remove it."

There was a brief silence, no one wanted to say any more for that moment, they were just glad they were alive after that ordeal.

Just then a plume of smoke from a chimney outside found its way into the room via an open window. From the smoke appeared Bug-a-Boo, looking glad to see everyone and carrying a large silk bag. "Good day," Bug-a-Boo cried, with a fluent bow and extruding an air of happiness and good cheer. "I'm happy to see you all well."

Zach sent a glare.

"I apologize for disappearing right before arriving in Bathill, but I had to make a visit to some interested parties about this matter," the wizard explained.

"Kina knows we're here," Alice protested, dryly.

"Not Kina. A certain man with a jolly demeanour who has been assisting me with a request I made shortly after you three were brought here."

Zach rolled his eyes. "You expect me to buy that Santa Claus has some interest in all this."

"I expect you to buy anything," Bug-a-Boo fired back at Zach. "You've been though probably the most cliché of hero's journey's and have seen magic performed before your eyes. Whether to believe or not is none of my concern. You are a grown man who is perfectly capable of coming to his own conclusions."

Ed laughed, but stopped when he felt the side of his face flare up in pain.

"Ah! Ed, my boy!" the wizard announced. "I come with a gift from the Master Smith of the North. When he heard about your eye, he made you this."

Bug-a-Boo produced from the bag a black box and lifted the lid to reveal an ivory eyeball with a sapphire iris and an ebony pupil.

"Now," Bug-a-Boo went on, "I've placed a charm on it so you'll be able to use it like a normal eye. We tried to find a stone that would match your eye colour, but sapphire was the closest. It shouldn't be too noticeable once it's inserted."

"Thank you," Ed replied.

"Now, as for you three," Bug-a-Boo continued, "I don't normally do this, but once Ed wanted you all to visit, I set to work fashioning these for you. I also had to get permission from my teacher, the Great Wizard Bandersnatch, before even considering passing them on to you three."

The old wizard handed Zach, Travis and Alice each a black box that was held closed with a brass clasp. Inside each of them was a small press bell, just like the one Ed used the first night he appeared.

"These bells," Bug-a-Boo explained, "will allow you to travel between worlds, or call on me when needed."

"I thought giving a person the power to cross worlds was a dangerous thing," Travis pointed out.

"I felt it was a worthy duty for Ed to provide his closest friends the ability," The old wizard explained. "Plus, you all proved yourselves very worthy of the right after saving everyone from Spyrus."

"You're a regular *Deus ex Machina,* Bugs," Zach put in.

"I wouldn't use that," Bug-a-Boo replied, trying not to blush. "Now, whenever you to are ready to go, all you need to do is press the button on the bells and you will be bought back home. I recommend aiming for a few minutes after you left your world for this one, that way no one will be the wiser to the matter."

"And what about my nicks and scrapes?" Zach queried. "People are going to wonder about stuff like that."

"Ah! My little Zach, if you are as smart as Ed claims you should be able to come up with something. I don't expect any of you keep secrets, though I do hope you will take a moment of *sober* thought before doing so. After all, you already know a wizard can be unpredictable."

With those last words, Bug-a-Boo gave a curt bow, walked to the window, and jumped into the smoke still billowing from the neighbouring building.

"I guess this is goodbye," Ed said at last, with a forlorn look.

"Not really," Travis said, assuring him. "We will always come back."

"It's fine," Ed went on. "I've been hung up on leaving you guys, but now I can see that you three are always going to be there at the end of line when needed."

It was a very teary goodbye. Ed hugged every single person despite the pain he was in, and thanked Zach, Alice and Travis for coming with him into the Faerie Lands. Once everyone had said their goodbyes, the trio pressed their bells and disappeared from the hospital room, leaving Ed alone. Ed wasn't sad though. Far from it.

www.ingramcontent.com/pod-product-compliance
Lightning Source LLC
LaVergne TN
LVHW041637060526
838200LV00040B/1605